UNTIL THE SUN RISES

Winston Gieseke (Editor)

UNTIL THE SUN RISES

Gay Vampire Erotica

BRUNO GMÜNDER

1st edition
© 2014 Bruno Gmünder Group GmbH
Kleiststraße 23-26, D-10787 Berlin
info@brunogmuender.com

Cover design: Steffen Kawelke
Cover photo: © 2014 George Duroy, USA
belamionline.com (Model: Dolph Lambert)
Printed in Germany

ISBN 978-3-86787-691-9

More about our books and authors:
www.brunogmuender.com

CONTENTS

INTRODUCTION:
GOOD TO THE LAST DROP

What's so alluring about the undead? Is it their charm? Their elegance? Or the fact that they know how to use their mouths?

Whatever the reason, vampire fetishes are as timeless and immortal as vampires themselves. And as diverse. From the terrifying Draculas of Bram Stoker and F.W. Murnau to the sexy heartthrobs of *Buffy the Vampire Slayer* and *The Vampire Diaries,* neck nibblers are the archetypal bad boys—powerful, intelligent, beautiful creatures that are arrogant and predatory, live by their own rules, and are immune to mortal fears like death, heights, or blood. They're also incredibly romantic beings who understand the art of seduction and generally won't ruin the moment by talking too much.

Plus they love necking.

Featuring explicit tales from some of gay erotica's most prolific and acclaimed authors, *Until the Sun Rises* overflows with kinky scenarios of thirsty vampires who are eager for a taste of more than your blood. While any vampirologist will tell you that our nocturnal neighbors can have various cravings—from a victim's life energy or emotions to the earth's elements—up front here, of course, are those in search of some serious monster mashing.

Often labeled incubi or pranic vampires, these sex-driven night stalkers with considerable mileage (Come on, who wouldn't want a guy who's had hundreds of years of practice?) know how to bring out the best in us. "The irony that fucking a dead man made him feel alive did *not* escape him," writes Pink Rushmore of Jack, a lovestruck mortal in "Twice Shy." A similar resurrection is experienced by Riley, the deeply depressed virtual shut-in in Gregory L. Norris's "In the Casket," and Phil, the frustrated screenwriter in Landon Dixon's "Movie Monster Mayhem!"

Some of the stories in this collection depict the sexy frivolity of a vampiric fling (Rob Rosen's "Little Sucker" and Michael Bracken's "Moon Doggie and the Nightsurfers at Hammerhead Beach") while others warn against the dangers of such an encounter. Whether these jugular junkies are offering us something we desperately want, as evidenced by Tommy in Vincent Lambert's "The Coming Storm" and Zach in David Aprys's "Irresistible," or they're just so desirable—like Alain in P.A. Friday's "Inhuman Ecstasy"—that we're temporarily blind to the risks of involvement, these tantalizing tales often leave us with lingering questions about our own depraved erotic wishes.

For example, when your boyfriend gets off with one of the living dead, should that be considered cheating? It's not like he'll bring home any diseases. That is, if he comes home at all. Sometimes a romp with an ancient bloodsucker can even bring people closer together, as is the case in Mark Wildyr's "Black Snow" and Brett Lockhard's "Shade of Night." For others—like the insatiable Leo in Ryan Field's "Sexual Transitioning"—a carnal binge is actually *necessary* to ensure a stable eternity. Or survival in the event of a zombie apocalypse, as evidenced in Chip Masterson's "Swarm."

The reason we're so turned on by these crimson tide connoisseurs is simple: Vampires embody all the traits that we find desirable. They're sexy, virile, and forever young—frozen in time at their sexual peak. They have a flair for seduction, an eagerness to penetrate with more than their eyes, and an insatiable need to suck things. (And they swallow, rather than spit.) Plus, they make us feel wanted. After all, their libidos and youth are rejuvenated by our blood and our spirit—and to get it, they're not afraid to use their charm and massive strength to overpower us. (So long as we first invite them in.)

And if that's not enough of an incentive, dating a vampire always leaves your days free.

Enjoy.

Winston Gieseke
Berlin

IN THE CASKET

Gregory L. Norris

In the weeks before the new tenant moved in to the big old house next door, shadows gathered around Riley and he fell into a state of deep depression. A spell of brisk rain cut the summer short, conjuring ugly, waxy mushrooms across the lawn. The normally bright colors inside Riley's New Englander lost their luster even when the lights were on, and sadness crept in through the windows and past the threshold.

Riley locked the front door in a town where few did. He started an odd pattern of going to bed earlier and sleeping in later, and dreamed strange scenarios about the past decades of his twenty-seven years of living and mostly ignored his present, which was steeped in gauzy mist and smothered by a growing sense of melancholy.

And then late one night he noticed a light coming from the back bedroom of his closest neighbor, a light where none should be. The big green house with the cream-colored shutters had sat vacant for the better part of two years. The previous renters were partiers who'd savaged the place and left behind enough trash to fill two dumpsters. Riley blinked; calcified sleep stung at his eyes. He pinched at their corners and sat up. The light from outside endured, no figment from a dream unwilling to end.

That side of the bed, the right, was only a few steps from the window. Months earlier in that time from another life when he still had a sense of humor, Riley often joked to himself—there was nobody else to yuck it up with in his modest home on Maple Street—that one wrong step and he'd spill through the window, roll down the section of metal roof above the sun porch, and keep on tumbling. Down the driveway, the road, and into the river, never to be seen again. During the maudlin weeks at the end of summer, the joke wasn't as funny as it had been at the beginning. He wondered if all depressed single people thought up ever more terrifying scenarios about death and dying alone.

The cold hardwood floor tickled Riley's soles. Dressed only in a pair of black boxer-briefs that hugged his body with unpleasant tightness, he moseyed over to the window and opened the drapes. The red velvet panels that denied the sun entrance on the rare mornings when it visited parted, and Riley gazed through bleary eyes at the other house's back bedroom.

The room, empty of artwork and furniture, glowed under the glare of a bald bulb on the ceiling-mounted fixture. Rain plunked, striking the leaves of the big oak at the corner of his backyard and the metal roof. The notes played a sad instrumental soundtrack. At some point in the long seconds that followed, Riley realized his dick was stiff. He gave it a squeeze. Pins and needles rippled in concentric circles, engulfing the rest of his flesh. A shiver teased the nape of his neck. He fought it, failed. Before him was an empty room in an abandoned house.

Maybe the owner had visited to check out the state of the place and had forgotten to switch off the lights. Or someone had broken in. It was also possible that Riley was still asleep and dreaming.

Dreaming, sure. Perhaps he'd dreamed through the entire month of August—dreamed the days now stacked up into weeks of going through motions, aware of the coffee but not its taste, eating dinner but not because he was hungry, just out of habit. Maybe he was a corpse and didn't yet know it—he'd croaked alone in his house, his fortress, and was cursed to Limbo, land of lost souls. He sure felt dead.

Then movement stirred in the empty room. A figure entered and moved directly beneath the bare light bulb—a man. If he was dreaming, Riley mused with a humorless chuckle, he didn't want to wake up.

The man looked older than Riley, with short, dark hair in a neat cut and a face beyond the definition of classically handsome. As Riley's breaths came with increasing difficulty, he agreed the man was almost painful to behold because he was so insanely hot. Pale blue dress shirt was unbuttoned and hanging open, exposing a treasure trail of dark fur that cut him down to—

Still asleep, he had to be! This was simply one last dying gasp of lust manifested in an X-rated dream about to end wet, Riley thought. He was really asleep on his stomach, grinding his cock into the mattress in an attempt to rub out a nocturnal load. Only he caught himself sucking down air and conscious of the world around him in strokes too concrete to be abstract. His new neighbor was naked apart from the shirt. Riley's eyes locked on the lush pelt of pubic hair beneath the man's defined abs. Lower, on the meaty dick hanging half-hard over two loose balls, the right sagging lower than its twin on the left. As Riley stared, the man's magnificent cock thickened fully without the help of a single stroke.

The man shuffled closer, his image cut off at the knees by the sill, the rest of his magnificence framed by the window. Riley forced his gaze up to see the man's vibrant blue eyes aimed back at him. Panic trumped lust. The drapes fell back in place. Riley stumbled away and landed on his spine atop the bunched bedclothes. Electricity pulsed through his blood, the spark originating at his cock. So handsome! The *handsomest* he'd ever crossed paths with.

The red velvet drapes mocked him, obstructing his view into the wonderland beyond the sun porch roof. The rain fell, its music in counterpoint against the rapid drum solo of his heartbeat. The organ had jumped out of his chest and into his cock, which had alchemized from flesh to steel.

"What the fuck …?" Riley whispered out loud to the lonely room.

An answer came from somewhere beyond, not in words but energy and dark emotion. His dripping cock attempted to take aim at the window like a divining rod attracted to water, held back only by the cotton noose of his boxer briefs. Curiously, Riley choked down a heavy swallow to find his mouth had gone completely dry. On his feet again, he maneuvered toward the drapes, drawn forward by his erection. Every cell in Riley's body now served his cock. He was *all* cock.

Riley reached the window. In a daze, he pulled the drapes aside. Light from the other house spilled in and, long last, the gloom that had smothered the world for weeks lifted.

"*Yes,*" Riley groaned, and smiled.

Days earlier, as the rain robbed the world of color and turned the inside of the house as well as the view outside into ashy shades of gray, Riley'd opened his yearbooks from school and jerked off to black and white photographs of his Western Civ teacher, gym teacher, and an endless succession of former classmates—faces and names he wouldn't have remembered otherwise.

Pumping his dick to old yearbook photos? Riley realized he'd surrounded himself with ghosts. Worse, his life force drained, he'd become one himself.

A man. In the house next door. In the window.

Riley rolled over. Sunlight streamed through the opened drapes.

The heavy red velvet fabric ballooned, stirred by a warm breeze that kept the dreamy smile on his lips.

He jolted up, caught the stale sweat smell, that of sex between men, only to plummet back down, a drop that felt like falling into a bottomless pit. The room spun. Riley's cock pulsed. Sliding his right hand down, he found where all the blood draining from his face had gone. Outside in the oak tree, a mourning dove cooed its sad song.

Eyes closed, Riley's smile widened. He stroked his cock and relived the details.

The drapes opened. The man—so handsome that it hurt to gaze directly at him, like staring too long at the surface of the sun—was still there. He flashed a cocky smirk that showed a length of clean white teeth, the gesture more snarl than actual smile. One big hand worked his cock, pumping the shaft up and down and forcing the head out from moist folds of foreskin. He tugged at his nuts with the other.

Unable to look away, Riley sighed, *"Fuck."*

His next sip of air proved almost impossible, as breathing was no longer easy or even involuntary. Unconsciously, he licked his lips. The man in the house next door offered a tip of his chin, that universal gesture between males that makes instant buddies out of strangers. He'd noticed Riley, acknowledged him—only the man's expression seemed equal parts hungry and horny.

The man stroked his thickness. Wetness glistened on the head and foreskin, its glow in the light of the bare bulb steadily hypnotizing Riley's eyes. The ever-present music from the rain waned; all he heard was the liquid telltale beat of his own heart.

Riley groped his erection and worked it free of his underwear. It wouldn't take much for him to shoot. And when he busted, it would be with the full force of the best nuttings of his life—and then some.

15

Up and down, he watched the man's performance, matching the strokes.

What the fuck was going on, and how was this possible?

He thought the questions, but somehow they jumped out of his skull and past Riley's lips.

"I'm here because you need me … and I need you," the man said, his voice a husky baritone. Sexy, it matched the rest of his components.

Riley blinked, and suddenly the man was directly outside his window, perched on the metal roof with cat-like grace. *Impossible,* Riley thought.

"Open up and invite me in," the man said.

Riley froze. Rain lashed the man's body. Up close, the full perfection of his limbs and muscles came clearly despite the broken quality of the light from the other house.

"How did you—?" Riley asked.

The man smiled. His cock pulsed left to right between his legs, moving under its own power. The man's balls flexed, too, his meaty tanks puffing visibly as the muscles of his dick exerted pull.

"Open up now," the man said, "or I'll look for another companion."

Their eyes again connected. The man's glowed with preternatural luminescence, like those of a wild predator caught in the glow of a car's headlights out on some desolate country road. Blue, the color of summer skies and morning glories and precious sapphires, only electrified. And unavoidable.

"No—stay," Riley said, and raised the window.

Light of a kind filled the room. An undercurrent of energy thrummed through the air, mimicking Riley's pulse, only from a bigger heart. A cosmic engine, he thought in that last rational moment before the man was there beside him. No, he wasn't simply a man but a force of nature. The cosmic engine was housed in his cock.

"Yes," the man said. He cupped Riley's chin in one big hand and gazed upon him like his was the most attractive face in the history of the world.

His other guided Riley's touch to the prize between his legs. Invisible fire crackled over Riley's fingertips, unleashing more cold than heat. Their mouths pressed together. The man's lips deepened the chill. Then Riley was on his knees beside the bed, high from the scent of rain on the man's skin, and none of his worries over the rest of the details challenged his excitement. For the first time in too long, Riley felt alive.

Sunlight streamed down. Through the splinters and spokes of gold, Riley relived the encounter in sips: rain-soaked shirt, smelling of the storm and the man's natural scent, dropping to the floor beside large bare feet, lush leg hair, and those wild eyes when Riley glanced up.

In the morning, with sunshine spilling into the room and pins and needles gossiping over his flesh, Riley reached down and found his cock at its hardest mast, eager for attention. He gave it a pump. Pre-cum oozed between his fingers, making spit or other lubrication unnecessary. Riley sucked in a deep sip of air, held it, and then just as deeply released the bottled breath. A lusty grin formed on his lips.

Riley remembered.

He took the other man's cock into his mouth.

One hand on fur-covered leg muscles, Riley's other was full of balls, gently tugging, rolling stones around in their hairy sac. The fullness pressed on his tongue in response. The taste of his handsome night visitor's flesh, salty at its tip, killed the last of his doubt.

Riley sucked the man's dick, and the invisible weight stacked onto his shoulders over the years evaporated. A lightness washed through him. If not for the man's dick between his lips and his hand on the back of his head, keeping him grounded, Riley imagined his body

17

levitating off the floor. Through the bedroom window, fulfilling that scenario … only instead of tumbling down, down to the river, he'd float up into the turbulent night sky.

It was OK to provide oral sex to this man, perfectly acceptable in the greater scheme of things to lick his balls, to hunger for his feet, his ass, his seed. Lightning crackled in the distance and thunder boomed, but the world didn't topple off its axis and the gods didn't unleash their rage upon the rest of the universe because one male showered affection on another's dick. As he attempted to deep-throat the man's cock all the way to the balls, it struck Riley that the only damned soul in the room was his, and he'd condemned it through so many years of denial.

A dream—this had to be a scenario playing out of his imagination, the most elaborate dream ever. Dreams could be liberating, and this one gave him permission to tongue behind the man's meaty nuts, to bury his nose in the lush curls wreathed around his dick, to suck harder, faster, savoring the taste of his cock-sock and knowing the man was quickly growing close to climaxing. Riley also knew he would swallow down the load once it squirted across his tongue— because none of this was real.

The man tensed and drove his dick in fully. A grunt sounded overhead in counterpoint. Wetness sprayed the roof of Riley's mouth. He gulped it down. A dream, nothing more.

"Oh fuck, yes!" the man groaned.

Several additional shots followed. At one point, the hand on the back of Riley's skull reached lower, grabbed him around the shoulder, and drew him back to his feet. Riley's eyes again fell into the gravity of the man's hypnotic blue gaze. A shiver tripped down his spine.

The man crushed his mouth over Riley's. They kissed. The pressure from Riley's dick, now stabbing into the meat of the man's spent erection, and the knowledge that the handsome stranger willingly tasted himself on their damp kisses, teased him to the edge. But before Riley's dick started to shoot, the man's mouth slid from cheek to throat. Electricity cascaded over Riley's flesh. The man sucked at tender skin, harder and with greater lust according to his rabid grunts. The scrape of teeth drew a moan from Riley's lips.

A hickey? Riley closed his eyes, right as the mildly painful jolts pushed his cock past the precipice.

He came again in the wash of morning sunlight. The wide smile on Riley's face persisted. A dream, yes. The best dream in history.

Riley slipped out of bed and moseyed into the upstairs bathroom to wash his hands. Standing half-hard, his eyes drifted toward the mirror above the sink and, for a startling instant, his reflection seemed only half there. He blinked, and his naked body solidified in front of his eyes, enough for him to notice the bruise on his throat, a purple blemish with four raised scabs, perfectly spaced like bite marks.

He wandered back into the bedroom to see that the window facing the empty house was open.

Riley paced. If those two elements of the previous night were real, had the rest of it happened? He scratched at the beard that had started out as day-old scruff weeks earlier and steadily thickened over the course of the summer's end.

A light where none should be. A man in a house where nobody lived. And what a man at that!

A man. Riley choked down a dry swallow and reached for the sweating glass on the counter. The rush of bubbles drove out his discomfort enough and allowed him to think. He touched his throat. Riley's dick twitched in his loose-fit cotton jogging shorts. Heat soared around him, reminding him of the fullness of his balls, which hung heavy without the constriction of underwear.

The man couldn't be real. The memory of the dream—if it was a dream—pushed him back to full stiffness. Riley scratched at his nuts and adjusted his cock. His toes curled in his sneakers, and the day's temperature instantly doubled.

Riley's cock tempted him to stroke it and relive the encounter. But the strange details soon had his feet in motion. Out of the house, into the sunlight, and down the driveway. He crossed through the strip of neatly mown lawn on his side of the property line, past the big oak tree in the backyard, and then through the tangled overgrowth beyond.

The For Sale sign was where he expected to find it—You're Invited to take a Look Inside it read beneath an Internet address for a virtual tour. Riley marched past the sign and up the front steps, aware of his tick-tocking erection. He knocked. Nobody answered. Riley's heart hammered in his ears. He knocked again, reached down to adjust his crotch, and winced. After standing at the door for another minute that felt more like an hour, he gave up and plodded home.

He'd always known he was attracted to men, but growing up in a conservative family Riley learned to keep the truth close to his heart. Maybe the intense desire for male companionship he'd walled up behind emotional brick and mortar had finally caused him to snap. There was no man in the house next door—the handsome demon-angel was simply a figment created by a mind that had lived in the closet too long and gone crazy over guilt and regret.

A balmy summer breeze swept through the house. Riley struggled to breathe, aware of his erection and the building pressure. Both the depression and the storm were over, the rain gone. Color and light had returned to the world. An illusion of happiness, too. But at what cost?

Night swept over the town. Riley ascended the stairs and plodded into his bedroom. At the back window, he opened the drapes. The house beyond sat dark. He stared and waited. Riley's cock pulsed. He groped its thickness and again heard the cadence of his heartbeat, broadcast out of his body and into the shadows.

A light switched on in the room across from his. Riley moaned a breathless, *"Fuck,"* and worked his fingers into his shorts. Wide eyes scanned the room's bare walls for any sign of life. A flash of motion flickered from the periphery—there one moment, gone the next.

"Riley," growled a masculine baritone.

For a second or so, Riley couldn't be sure if the voice was real or only inside his head—wishful thinking and further proof he'd come undone. Then he turned and froze. Blue eyes glowed in the dark. The man's body materialized around them.

"You," Riley gasped. "You're real!"

The man stepped closer. Riley attempted to match him in retreat. The backs of his legs met the windowsill. Warm air surged up, a reminder of the drop to the roof below and the danger of falling, falling, dying beyond.

The man's lips formed a crooked smile. "Very real. My name's Derek."

"How did you get in here?"

"You invited me."

The drapes billowed. Riley stepped away from the window, and he and the handsome intruder did a slow circle that again put Riley near the bed.

"Do you want me to go?"

Riley sucked down a breath and smelled the seductive scent of the intruder's skin. The man—a magnificent demigod—folded his arms and waited for an answer. Riley saw that his visitor's chest was bare.

"I—" he stuttered.

"If you don't want me here, just say so."

"Did you bite my neck?" asked Riley.

"Did you suck my dick?" Derek countered, his voice cool and confident, matching his grin. "Because if you did, we both got exactly what we wanted."

Derek uncrossed his arms and stepped forward.

"What we *needed*."

Riley's feet tangled. He dropped onto the bed. Derek strutted up to him, and he saw the other man's magnificent body was as bare beneath the waist as above. Derek's cock metronomed back and forth at its hardest, head protruding fully from a ring of damp foreskin. Riley's mouth watered.

"I heard your sadness, felt the hurt in your heart, and thought we should help one another. I know what you need."

Riley forced his eyes back up to Derek's. "Heard my sadness? What are you?"

"I can offer you a chance to forget all your ridiculous guilt, to explore and enjoy every one of your secret lusts," Derek said. "I can give you happiness. But only if you want it."

Riley considered the man's words without comment. Derek shrugged and turned toward the window, his bare feet whispering across the floor, as though levitating just above the hardwood.

"Wait," Riley called. In the seconds he struggled to get the word past his lips, Riley saw himself lost in the house, only partially there. A living ghost. Alone.

Derek halted and spun around. The other man flashed a sharp smile on his return to the bed. He seized Riley's face in his hands and crushed their mouths together. Riley's racing pulse jumped out of his body and drummed through the heat and darkness. Mouths locked. Hands groped. Derek freed him of what little covered his body, and their cocks wrangled like their tongues.

The kiss broke. Derek straightened and guided his dick toward Riley's lips.

22

Riley woke in a pool of sunlight. He licked his lips and tasted the dregs of Derek's nectar. Riley's cock pulsed in response. He briefly groped his dick before fingers wandered back up to his throat. His smile widened.

He slipped out of bed and padded naked down the stairs, aware of the lightness in his steps. He paused at the door to the basement. There, Derek's voice played in his thoughts.

I need an assistant who will protect me during the daylight. In exchange for your loyalty, I promise to protect you and care for all of your needs as well.

"Derek," he sighed.

Riley closed his eyes and jerked his cock. He couldn't remember a morning when he'd felt happier. A dead man had brought him back to life.

SHADE OF NIGHT

Brett Lockhard

Through the window Ethan looked past the full branches of the giant oak. Beyond it the azure sky was expansive and hopeful. He lingered here, his mind quiet, relishing the tranquility of the cottage he had rented with his partner Jack, who slept beside him. These were halcyon minutes, his eyes soft in the early day, the sunlight gentle as it splashed into the bedroom. All of it belied the first of the season's leaves beginning to yellow outside, a harbinger of what was to come.

Waking up slowly next to him, Jack dragged his hand through the hair of Ethan's broad chest, and the touch of it sent his cock surging within seconds. He felt the ridges of Ethan's indomitable abs and looked up to admire the creases that had just started forming around his deep set green eyes. He reached for Ethan's monster-thick cock—a thing of so much rank fantasy over the years, a thing that now proved useful on mornings like these, mornings that accommodated the passion that still tore through him after all this time together.

With not a word yet spoken, Jack kissed a path through the soft fur of Ethan's stomach and finally, gratefully, stopped to inhale the warm musk of the man's pubes. His tongue made a familiar pass around the head of Ethan's nine-inch cock. He licked carefully at first, wetting the entire tip and an inch of the shaft, pulling back to tease him, then approaching again, this time sucking but still only at the head. Ethan watched intently, excited by the way his pre-cum stretched from Jack's lips when he pulled away. He waited for the predictable surge that told Jack it was time to take it all. Ethan's cock head swelled, unfathomable though it might seem to grow even bigger, and Jack dove hungrily on it. Ethan liked to watch as the inches disappeared. Reaching the back of the throat, he waited for Jack's steadying inhale through the nose, then thrust his hips forward for a single final plunge into the gorge.

Jack froze for a second, seizing around the gargantuan member choking him. He allowed the tip to recede from his throat, then impaled himself again and again with it. He made gurgling sounds, deftly sneaking in air between deep swallows of the outsized pole. Skilled though he was, Jack was lightheaded already. Ethan let his head drop backward, reveling in the sounds of slobbering, then lifted it again to make contact with Jack's intense, adoring eyes. He reached forward and grabbed a thatch of his partner's black hair. At thirty-six, Jack still boasted a mess of youth at his crown—as much a sign of virility as his unyielding square jaw and the black stubble that shadowed his face.

Jack pulled back, gliding his slick upper lip over the throbbing head. As he crested the tip, Ethan's cock slapped against his rock-hard abs with a thud. Using his hand for the first time, Jack grabbed the shaft and went intently to work on bringing Ethan to orgasm.

"You want my cum?" Ethan asked. "Or should I save it for your ass?"

"Give it to me now," Jack said, his first words to Ethan today. "I can't wait for it."

With that, Ethan gripped the edge of the mattress, which was now exposed where the sheet had slid off. He snarled, possessed by something close to pain, an anguished climb to orgasm. Jack lifted his eyes to watch while he waited eagerly for the flood. With a gasp, Ethan released in four distinct shots. Allowing his mouth to fill before swallowing, Jack closed his eyes and enjoyed the taste on his tongue. Despite his own cock still hard and twitching, Jack felt relief himself when the wad of cream coated his throat as he finally took it all down.

Ethan's heavy cock rested on Jack's tongue. With a final squeeze, Jack milked the remains and licked the cock clean before collapsing on Ethan's furry chest.

"You want it now?" Ethan asked.

"I want to stay here for a minute," Jack replied. With his head resting on Ethan's chest, Jack heard the slow, sure beat of his heart.

Ethan ran his hand through Jack's hair and felt the sharp dark stubble that Jack wore with effortless masculine appeal. There could be nothing more to ask than this—to be naked in the sunlight with a drained cock and the person he loved at his chest. Ethan looked outside and noticed, even late into the fall, the colors still seemed so saturated, so full of life. And still, Ethan could not help thinking about what lie ahead—the sky a heavy November gray, the last of the lingering leaves quivering on its branch, then floating off in a cold wind.

Jack traced a finger along Ethan's obliques, muscles he was astonished to find still, now that they were men for whom age thirty-five was a memory. At the hipbone, Jack swept two fingers across the waistline, then descended to where the hair of Ethan's lower abs tangled with the pubes in which Jack wanted again to bury his face. But he wanted something now even more. When he reached for Ethan's cock, he found all nine inches ready for him. He leaned forward to feel Ethan's warm breath on his lips. He asked with only his eyes, and Ethan nodded encouragingly to go ahead. So little needed to be said between them.

As Jack adjusted the head of Ethan's cock at the rim of his ass, he was grateful for a partner like this, someone with such unyielding sexual interest in him. Losing inch after inch into the warm maw, Ethan was mesmerized by the sight of the man above him. From the rugged lines of his jaw to the cut ledges of his chest covered with fur, in silhouette he could have been twenty-seven years old. On display here was the power of his manhood but none of the physical decay Ethan might have expected, years ago, thinking about the approach of middle age. Now fully inside, Ethan felt the sweet contact of Jack's firm ass against his hips. As he began to thrust, Jack's ass welcomed him fully. Now in a steady, mindless wave, Jack let sound the grunts and satisfied pleas of a man who was now complete. And Ethan, in the midst of easily bestowing such pleasure, had one overriding thought: *It won't be like this forever.*

Soon there would be the decline. There would be no predicting when it started exactly. But once set in motion, things would not reverse. He imagined the future—not a bad one, a wager could be made on that. But even as Ethan's thrusts intensified, a quiet sadness grew within him. Nothing in this world would be forever, and realizing it was desperation.

Above Ethan, Jack locked his canon arms to brace against the torrent of the gigantic cock. He moaned pleadingly as the fucking grew more intense, and Ethan clutched at his partner's biceps, squeezing around the bulging veins that spoke of all those early morning river rows, that pulsed with the vitality and the ecstasy of a man in his prime.

Ethan kept time with Jack's gasps, imparting the euphoria of this seminal fuck, all the while registering the creeping feeling of fear. The tears were near the surface as Ethan sat up and reached his substantial arms around the man he could not possibly love more. He held him tight as he threw him on his back, never pulling his cock out of the grateful ass.

As the sounds of Ethan's pounding reached crescendo, Jack let loose a protracted moan of uncontrolled yearning. It was an orgasm that came from deep within, as though every cell in his body joined in creating the surge of power that erupted through his cut eight-incher.

Ethan felt the hot spill against his lower abs and slowed his pace until he was completely still, pressing his firm body, now wet with sweat, against Jack's. Together their scent was a stinging brine, a smell that told of the basest acts, a smell they alone could appreciate. Ethan nestled his face in Jack's neck and kissed him warmly, noticing the strong post-fuck pulse of the jugular against his tongue. The two incredible bodies now one, Ethan did not move. With his large cock still throbbing in Jack's ass, Ethan simply held him tightly, their faces now pressed together, his breath suspended as if stopping time. Overcome now, Ethan felt the first tear escape. With his big arms around Jack's chest, he squeezed tighter, feeling this might be the closest two people had ever been. He radiated from the core as he fired three enormous wads into Jack's hole.

There was silence then. The two men lay together, lost in the prolactin flood, knowing no need except to remain like this with each other. "Does it get any better?" Jack asked. "Or should we just be done now, knowing we've had it all?"

Jack was joking, of course—but Ethan recognized some truth in the question. This life would have nothing more for them than this moment, than right now being in each other's arms. And really how was it possible to go on knowing that the rest of life would be only fractional pleasures doled out like soup at a shelter? Ethan merely stroked Jack's hair, unable to entertain these questions. "I love you," he said, lifting his head to kiss Jack's parted lips.

Eventually the day began—with a trip to the little market in town where they would pick up some food for the next few days. They were not really Hamptons people; they didn't have a house or a beach club out here—not for lack of means, but for lack of desire. The pretense, the parties, it just wasn't their scene. But if something required their presence, they were game for a few days at a time. They rented the same cottage on a gravel path in Bridgehampton and felt comfortable returning to it when needed. At the very least, the time away reminded them how good their sex was.

The reason for this particular weekend was to support a not-so-close friend's new film. To raise money for production, there would be a fundraiser hosted by a rich man everything about whom they knew only through rumors, some of which were rather dark. The invitation announced: SUNSET COCKTAILS AND SCREENING. DINNER TO FOLLOW.

Jack finished the knot of his tie in the bathroom mirror while Ethan, already fully dressed in a sports coat, jeans, and wingtip boots, sat patiently in the living room. Looking over the rim of his martini glass, Ethan noticed the sun was already low in the sky. A navy-purple cast was falling like a curtain on the closing day.

When he finished dressing, Jack poured himself a drink, joined Ethan on the couch, and looked out into the end of the day. In the quiet, he couldn't help thinking of them as two men growing old in their rocking chairs, the quiet of the house as much a companion to them as they were to each other.

They were among the first to arrive. Entering the stone Gothic manse, they found themselves alone in the marble foyer, unable to locate the sounds of the host or any guests.

"Welcome, gentlemen," the host, Anton, said, suddenly standing between the couple and the door. Jack shuddered when the silence broke. He turned to take in the imposing vision of this six-foot-three man with predatory obsidian eyes and hair that framed his face in dark waves. He was a dramatic vision of striking features and brute strength, not to mention something unknown and intoxicating.

The silk pocket square and oxford shoes were all polish, but the black hair that crept along substantial wrists, exposed only when the cuffs slid on his arms, was pure animal.

"I'm delighted to have you," Anton said. His gaze was mesmerizing.

Ethan extended his hand. "It's so good of you to have us." As their hands met, Ethan was aware of succumbing to whatever magic this man offered. Anton's grip was strong, his skin surprisingly cold to the touch. After too many seconds shaking hands, Ethan managed finally to pull his away. He turned to Jack: "Let's get a drink, shall we?"

Jack merely nodded. Ethan reached for his waist as they walked toward the game room, where antlers adorned broad-paneled walls and model servers made turns around the room with a waltz's grace. One of them bowed slightly as he offered flutes of pink champagne. As they sipped, Ethan peered through the windows. He noticed the final wisps of color disappearing on the horizon and then, finally, the deep blue shade of night pulled down like surrender.

In New York, Ethan and Jack were accustomed to pretty crowds, to rooms boasting an excessive style quotient. But as guests poured into the game room and spilled onto the balcony, it became clear this party was like nothing they had seen before. It was a parade of men, all in their early to mid-thirties, each more beautiful than the one before. The room became a phantasmagoria of sharp-lined jaws and piercing eyes, of broad chests and perfect skin, of flutes filled with and drained of varying pinks. As the men circled each other, it was a dance of hunter and prey. The night took on a palpable smoothness, which Jack attributed to the bubbles. For Ethan there was something more, and he was determined to discover it.

With his bourbon-liqueur voice poured into Ethan's ear, Anton put his hand on Jack's shoulder and said, "Join me in the theater, won't you?" As they turned to follow, Ethan's hand brushed Anton's. Perhaps just an accident, the body contact sprang Ethan's cock to life, tensing against the fabric of his briefs.

Ethan and Jack followed Anton to the back row of the theater, a room inside the house that could have passed for a legitimate box office cinema. Sitting between them, Ethan felt the unmistakable slick of pre-cum at the tip of his semi-hard cock. He put his hand on Jack's baseball-bat forearm, an attempt to convince himself it was his partner who had turned him on. Jack turned to kiss Ethan, smiled knowingly, then whispered, "My ass is still humming from that epic fuck this morning."

When Ethan returned to face forward, Anton leaned into his other ear: "I'm usually here watching, you know, art house films. It's nice to have visitors who want to see actual art being made."

The opening credits gave way to a grainy title screen, and "Canyon Shadows" floated across the celluloid. Produced on a $50,000 budget, the film was "a quiet masterpiece that teased light out of the most desperate corners of our world." That's what the *Village Voice* said about it anyway, when it debuted in Toronto.

"Do you like it so far?" Anton asked midway through.

"I think it's wonderful," Ethan said, now speaking directly to Anton's mouth, their faces mere inches from each other, instead of into his ear.

Anton took the tacit invitation to squeeze Ethan's upper thigh. Ethan uncrossed his legs and let their knees touch. Starting softly, Anton ran his finger deftly along the inside of Ethan's thigh. It was only because he was a doctor that Ethan recognized the path traced as his femoral artery.

Ethan's heart pounded in his chest. His cock ached as it pressed against the stiff zipper of his jeans. As if reading his mind, Anton let his fingers wander and, arriving at the impressive member, traced

31

the length of it until he reached the tip and then, fully the gentleman, returned his hand to his lap.

"I love this ending," Anton said to Ethan. The screen closed in on a man about to be found by his wife after a near-fatal car accident. He is bleeding on the side of the road. After embracing his listless body and kissing his face, the woman looks up and screams into the empty night, her face covered in blood. Next to Ethan, Anton lit up with an enormous smile. The final shot transitioned from the black night sky to the brightest white light, exposing the faces of the audience—a hundred expressions of revelry. A standing ovation, and Jack leaned over to Ethan and said, "Are you seeing …"

Interrupting him, Ethan said, "Uh-huh, yeah." In his pants, Ethan's cock leaked pre-cum uncontrollably now. "I have to go to the bathroom, Jack. You're OK, right? I'll meet you back in the game room? One more drink and then we hit the road?"

"Uh-huh."

"That was remarkable," Ethan said to Anton. "If you'll excuse me, I think I had a bit too much champagne."

At the end of a long corridor, Ethan found a bathroom that promised the three minutes of privacy he needed to get this done. It took all his willpower to stop and lock the door. Ripping his pants down with one hand, he used the other to begin stroking his enormous cock. The head was already wet with pre-cum, and his balls were boiling, ready to set free an unthinkable load. While yanking wildly, Ethan landed with a thud on the toilet seat and wrestled his pants to his ankles. Within seconds he found himself close to the brink. He breathed hard and bit his lip. Sitting up to grab toilet paper, he noticed the sudden appearance of a shadow through the door.

Ethan tended to doubt himself in situations like this; he was a doctor, after all—not the kind prone to beliefs in the supernatural. More than the uncanny appearance of this shadow, however, there was the immediate electric presence that charged the small room. It was un-yielding desire. It was a lifetime's worth of adrenaline revealed in a single wave of clarity, of unfathomable energy.

With his eye on the shadow, Ethan could not stifle the urgent moan of this satisfaction. It was a growl, almost, a beast's cry that started in the back of the throat. And then, of course, there were the heavy wads slung from his cock, one of which missed the toilet paper and landed squarely on his chin. Out of breath now, Ethan collected himself, taking more toilet paper to wipe his face, tucking in his shirt, zipping up. The orgasm yielded little in the way of relief. If anything, Ethan feared, it left him somehow wanting more. He watched the shadow intently as he reached for the doorknob. When he finally swung it open, Ethan confronted an empty hallway.

His senses now heightened, Ethan instinctively turned right, chasing the idea of Anton. The voices of the crowd faded behind him as he approached the master bedroom at the end of the hall. He thought he had seen someone move in the doorway as he entered, but found no one inside. Beginning to feel unwell now, he stepped outside to collect himself. He walked onto the terrace and kept going. Almost at the water, he rested his forearm on a tree and noticed, at the other end of the house, the golden light of the game room now filled with guests. *He must be there, too,* Ethan thought, wondering what he was hoping to get from finding Anton in the first place.

Shaking off the defeat, Ethan turned to head back inside. And there was Anton, as though waiting for him the whole time. "Did you get lost?" he asked, moving toward him.

"I needed some air," Ethan said, standing still.

"Tell me, what are you looking for?"

"You." Ethan said without hesitation. He had never been so sure of any word.

His hand suddenly on Ethan's neck, Anton leaned in as if to offer the most sensuous kiss. Ethan's mouth opened gently, his lips barely grazing Anton's. And then, without warning, Anton flipped Ethan around and had him pinned against the tree. In one precise movement, Anton unzipped Ethan and yanked his pants to the ankles, all while keeping his arms held firm against the tree.

Anton held one hand against Ethan's broad back while spreading apart the firm cheeks of his ass. He started gently, using the tip of his expert tongue to wet only the perimeter of Ethan's rim. The hole puckered anxiously as Anton built excitement by spiraling slowly toward his prize. He paused for a few silent seconds before plunging his tongue fully into the now-eager hole. Ethan made his first noise, a groan of concession that signaled to Anton he was ready for whatever was in store—not that Anton needed permission.

His body pressed against Ethan's, Anton was a force not to be questioned. Ethan bowed his head against the tree as Anton licked a path from his earlobe along the cords of his neck. Anton stopped at the shoulder and bit, careful not to break the skin—obvious that he was holding himself back.

Ethan breathed heavily, succumbing to the power of the creature behind him. He felt his feet kicked apart and then, within seconds, Anton skewered him with his incomparable cock. The night sky turned silver as Ethan's vision blurred. It had been years since Ethan had been fucked, and he could not remember a dick this size in real life—somehow bigger than his own, which had been called too big by more than a few partners. The force of the thing tearing into him took his breath away. With the entire tool now buried in Ethan, Anton paused in an act of mercy, waiting patiently in the bated silence for his ass to relax.

It took only seconds for Ethan's insides to soften, allowing even more of Anton into him. Feeling the last of his length vanish in

Ethan's hole, Anton rested his hairy forearm across his back and held his shoulder firmly.

The fury ensued. The strength of Anton's pounding was impossible to describe. All Ethan knew was that he wanted more of it. "Harder," he said.

"Are you sure?" Anton said, having never, in all his years, heard this request.

"Fuck. Me." He got a quick breath in. *"Harder."*

What followed was an impossible brutality that sent shocks through Ethan's body. It was clear now that he was no longer supporting himself against the tree. It was Anton who was holding him there. His moans lost all self-consciousness; there was no awareness of the party nearby. There was only the power of this thing inside him, the experience of Anton's primitive virility taking hold. He bellowed with a mixture of pure pleasure and the most exciting pain.

Anton threw Ethan to the ground and took a moment to appreciate the look of vitality in this man who wanted it all—with all the darkness that entailed. He directed the head of his cock against Ethan's aching hole. Ethan smiled, and Anton kissed him this time as he entered. Slowly at first, the cock slid in more easily this time. Ethan was thankful to be filled again by his powerful tool and now, unexpectedly, by his mouth at his nipple. Anton's teeth closed around the soft flesh, and Ethan soared, an electric current ripping through his torso and into his balls, which were already aching in anticipation.

"How is it for you?" Ethan asked, understanding fully what he was about to find out.

"What part?"

"What is it like?"

"It's like nothing you've ever experienced, Ethan. It's unyielding strength. Colors so vivid you want to cry. The end of everything you fear. But it's not for the faint of heart. Some find it lonely."

"Uh-huh," Ethan's head was grinding into the dirt and the grass, unable to control himself. "But not for everyone?"

"No. Not for everyone."

Ethan let out a roar of pleasure as Anton ripped through him again. His rock-hard cock expelled a pool of pre-cum on his stomach. Anton scooped some up, stretched it between his fingers, then put them deep in Ethan's mouth, feeding him and choking him at once.

"I want to feed you, too," Ethan said. Anton didn't say anything, just held him with his eyes. They were bound by a mutual understanding. "But Jack's still inside."

"I know," Anton said. "I know."

"Now," Ethan said.

Anton continued to pound Ethan's ass while taking his solid cock in his hand. With a confident grip, he timed the jerking of Ethan's cock with each slam against his ass. Ethan closed his eyes as if taken to another plane. A pleading moan filled the night as he came. And just as the first geyser erupted from his cock, Anton leaned forward, his fangs exposed now, and tore open the side of his neck.

In this moment, Ethan felt himself rise from his body. Around him the colors of night faded to gray and then, as though in a dream, what he saw was a flood of unfathomable radiance. The blood feast was an elegy to every pleasure, both of this world and another. And now that it was over, after Ethan's screams had subsided, there was quiet once again, broken only by the distant din of the party.

Anton took the appropriate measures, dressed himself and wiped his mouth as he stood up. He turned toward the house and saw a figure moving toward him in the shadows. They approached each other carefully. In the moonlight Jack's face became clear, but Anton managed to remain in the shadows.

"Anton, is that you?"

"Yes."

"I'm looking for Ethan. Have you seen him?"

"Come with me. I'll take you to him."

BIRTHDAY

Natty Soltesz

I was born when I was eighteen, the summer of 1997, in Ocean City, Maryland. I was there for Senior Week, a debaucherous rite of passage where freshly-graduated high school students soak up the sun when they're not drinking themselves stupid. It was our first taste of freedom from parental supervision before we headed to college. Except I never went to college and I never left Ocean City.

Before it happened, though—when I was still human, before I killed a person for the first time—I was sitting with Travis in a lifeguard chair on the beach in the dark early morning. We'd been talking about it all night. It was already decided. The vast, unreachable depths of the ocean lapped against the shore.

Travis took my hand. I looked at the water and thought about how he'd first approached me on this very beach. It was only a few days ago. I'd never even had sex with another guy then. And really, even though I'd had sex with Travis, I still hadn't had sex with another guy.

"How did you know I'd want to become one of you?" I said. "Could you sense something in me from the beginning?"

"No, not really," Travis said, staring off into the distance. His dark Italian features were what first drew me to him—thick hair that stood up from his head, bedroom eyes, and a joker's grin that spread across his face. "I didn't know you'd want to come over at all. At least not until we had sex. Then I could tell."

"So, why were you following me around? Did you just want to meet me?"

"Yes," Travis said, and looked me in the eye. "And also, I was thinking about killing you."

Travis got down from the chair and I followed. The sky was starting to brighten as we made our way back to the boardwalk, to Underworld, which was Travis's store. It was right on the boardwalk but tucked back along a corridor painted bright swirling psychedelic colors. He led me through the dark store, past racks of black rock T-shirts, posters, shelves of incense, and a case full of glass pipes.

We went through the tattoo room and into the door that went up to Travis's apartment, which was where I'd lost my virginity just two days before. Except we didn't go upstairs this time. Travis let the door shut behind us. We were in a foyer, mudroom. On the other side was a big metal door with a pressure bar that led outside.

"Step over here," Travis said, ushering me to one side. He lifted a rubber-bottomed rug from the floor. There was a square metal panel in the floor. He lifted it and set it against the wall. I looked down into the hole it had been covering. Stone steps that looked like they had been crudely carved out of the foundation of the building led into darkness. "Go ahead," Travis said—and for the first time I was truly afraid.

It smelled earthy: salty and damp. I descended until I was at the bottom. "I can't see anything," I said.

Travis came up behind me. "Sorry," he said. "I forget sometimes. One sec." He went around me and into the darkness, the sound of his

39

feet on the gritty floor echoed. I heard the crackle of a match being lit and Travis came from around a corner, holding a candle.

We were in a cavern. The walls and floor were dirt, smooth and packed down but still ragged, with roots hanging and jutting from the sides like reaching hands. "Come this way," Travis said.

I followed him and came into a wide, low-ceilinged room. The walls were draped in deep red and orange crushed velvet fabric and the floor was covered in swaths of carpet and oriental rugs. There were couches along the side, and while the cavern had seemed damp and cool, this room was dry and warm.

In the center of the room was a table—an altar. It had candles on it and Travis lit them one by one, making the room glow brightly.

"Sonny got into doing ritualistic stuff a couple decades back," Travis said, motioning to the altar. Sonny was one of them. He worked in the store. "We really don't use it anymore."

"Where is Sonny?"

"Just down the way," Travis said, motioning to the cavern. "It's morning. He's asleep." He motioned to the couch. "Sit."

Travis sat next to me. He put his arm around me and kissed me. I kissed him back. Somewhere outside the sun was rising. I wasn't ever going to see it again.

"Tell me why we're here," he said.

"You're going to make me like you."

"Right. I'm going to bring you over. When it's time, I'll bite into your jugular and suck out most of your blood. Then I'll feed you my blood and then it'll start."

"Will it hurt?"

"Yes. It's birth. Or death. It's coming over, to another plane. Which always hurts." Travis put a hand on my leg. We already talked about how this was forever, and about how in order to continue living I'd have to kill. He ran his hand up my leg. He began to seduce me like

40

he had all night. Except this time it was with his body. Earlier it had been with words.

Don't think about the hurt. Think about how wonderful it will be. You'll be impervious. You'll explore the world like nobody else can because you'll have nothing but time, and you'll live beyond their rules: self-imposed, government, morals. We're not governed by their gods.

He stopped his hand just short of my cock. Let it get hard with the anticipation of him touching it.

Even killing them can be beautiful. Because they really don't die, we are subsuming them. They're as immortal as we are, in a way. Their energy goes into us, fuels us. They die, yes, but the big lie is that death is the end.

He grabbed my crotch. I was hard. His face was close to mine and I thought he was going to kiss me again but he didn't—he just kept his face close and looked into my eyes. The soft sweetness of his breath wafted over me, and I looked at his soft lips and tongue and wanted to suck them, wanted them on mine. His eyes moved from my eyes to my neck and it occurred to me that maybe he was as afraid as I was, that he'd have to keep tight control over an instinct that told him just to feed. That it was as hard for the parent as it was for the child.

He stripped off my shirt, revealing my smoothly muscled chest. I had a warm tan from lying out in the sun all week. He had me stand and we stood next to each other. I could see his cock getting hard in his black pants. He took off my pants next, sliding them off my smooth thighs, taking them off one foot at a time. He lingered there by my feet, nuzzling his handsome face against the rising pole in my thin briefs, brushing his chin against it. I felt his warm breath on my hot cock through my underwear. He licked the tip of my cock where pre-cum was seeping through the fabric, and I saw his teeth, just a little. And they looked longer than before, sharper. Just a little.

He noticed me looking and he stood, putting his hand in my hair, pressing his hard crotch against mine, his stomach against mine.

There's a killing response that's just like sexual response. And even though I'm not going to kill you I'm still going there. Getting warmed up, turned on, holding off. Foreplay. The longer you hold off and build it up, the better it is. That's why when we kill we draw it out as much as we can, let it sit within us—the hunger, the painful wanting of it, the empty-stomached reality of our need. To feel your fangs straining like mine will be, the ache of stretching enamel and gums, the animal heart inside us pounding and dying to be expressed, waiting for that release, that moment of attack which is as mind-blowing as cumming.

He took off my briefs, released my hot cock into the cool air of the basement. I liked it—the vulnerability. I could be killed, I knew. He could lose control, change his mind, kill me and I'd be helpless.

He opened his mouth and took my cock into it. I felt the swipe of his teeth—not quite scraping, just gliding over it. Despite the fear or because of it, the pleasure was intense. He had a tight suction on my cock, and it felt like my cock was a straw and through it he could suck the cum right out of my nuts. Maybe he could?

He stood. "Take off my clothes now," he said.

I did as he said. Took off his shirt. His nipples hardened just like anybody else's when exposed to the cool basement air. I tweaked one, ran my hand across his hairy chest. I took down his underwear and lifted them off of his thick feet (patches of black hair on the tops of his toes). Then I felt up his hairy legs, calves, rounded thighs. His cock, thick as a tube of toothpaste, rose from his balls. I felt its heat next to my face. Lifted it in my hand, peeled it away from his nuts and took it in my mouth. I could taste his pre-cum. What was it for?

I licked my way up his stomach, which was trim but pleasingly thick, swirled with a sparser version of the thick, dark hair that swarmed around the top of his cock in a thicket. He smelled good.

Like a man. I licked his nipples and came up to his face. He was smiling, waiting for me.

He stood naked before me. He was glorious, his body strong and wide, his huge cock swinging back and forth in front of him like a pendulum. I thought that I might look like him one day, be like him, my body composition changing until we were the same person—or would we be? If our outsides changed, like Travis said they did, subtly shifting over the decades, looking older or younger or switching genders, did our insides change as well?

He smiled—a bashful, half smile—and turned around. Propped himself against the wall and spread his legs out a bit. His strong back was splayed wide, hands on the wall almost six feet apart. His back tapered down to a V, with a smattering of hair, wispy yet dark, trailing all the way down his lats, which were thick like sirloin steaks, and fanning out into a brush over his firm and perfect ass.

I embraced him from behind, wrapped my arms around his wide and warm chest and let my hard prick rest against the crack of his ass, which was so firm that my cock didn't really slip between his cheeks. I kissed the back of his neck and savored the smell of him, a deep masculine scent that wasn't quite human. I felt him relax his ass cheeks a little, allowing my cock to slip in between them. I could feel the heat of his hole against the head of my cock, deep inside.

We'd already had sex twice, and both times I'd been the one to get fucked. I thought I might cum just from slipping my prick against his hole but Travis knew what he was doing.

"Kiss your way down my back," he instructed. I licked muscles and hair. "Explore all over your dad's body. Do whatever you want with it." That was the first time he'd ever used the word "dad," the first time we used this sort of role-play. It turned me on instantly.

I kissed my way down his back, drawing my tongue along the curve of his spine, stopping when I got to the top of his butt crack.

"Play with Dad's butt. He likes that," he said. I laughed and it broke the tension a little. I tongued the tip of his crack and he moaned and pushed his ass back toward my tongue, revealing more wispy black hair and his pink asshole.

"Are you sure it's OK to do this?" I asked, my mouth hovering just over his hole. The smell was deep and masculine, like aged wood. He would tell me later about how it works, how our digestive systems, like most of our organs, become vestiges, useless images of what they were when we were human.

"Sure it is," he said. "Aren't you curious?" I was, and had been since he'd done it to me the night we first had sex. I licked a swath right up his crack and against his hole. His whole body shuddered. It didn't taste dirty at all.

I licked up his thighs and around the base of his ass cheeks, skimming around the fur and licking the slopes and curves. Travis moaned whenever my tongue came close to the slick and wrinkled skin of his hole.

We feel sex. We feel joy and happiness and sadness just like people but our lives are more practiced, longer lived. We're naive, then wise— then naive, then wise all over and over again. You really never stop learning things from this world. The longer you live, the more you realize you don't really understand any of it.

He pushed his ass back against my face. I dug my tongue deeply into his asshole. He squirmed back to meet it and groaned loudly. It seemed to echo down the dark cavern. I still didn't know where that cavern led.

"Slide a finger inside me. Get it wet first. Go easy on me, it's been a while."

"Will it hurt?"

"No. It's gonna feel great for both of us. I'll show you exactly how, how to make Dad's ass feel good." He turned around and smiled back at me, the sharpness of his teeth shining in the low candlelight. It was easy to forget what was going to happen, he was so boyish and playful about it.

He draped himself belly-first onto the sofa, his left leg dangling on to the floor, perfect firm butt parted. He rested his head on his arms and closed his eyes like it was all a beautiful dream. I licked him some more like that, loving the way the tip of my tongue caught right into his hole like it was snapping at me, hungry for more. "Get your finger nice and wet and slide it inside."

I did as he said, pressing my wet finger to the muscled ring of his hole and pressing in. The tip popped inside. Travis gasped. It was tight but I felt him adjust himself as I slid it inside, contracting and relaxing his muscle. The more he relaxed the more he drew my finger into him until I was in him up to my knuckle. "Deeper," he said.

Soon he asked for a second finger. I felt his cock as I pressed my two fingers together and pushed them into him. His cock got harder as I stretched him open. He groaned.

"I'm ready for your cock, now," he said.

"Should we use a condom?"

"No need."

Viruses can't do a lot in our bodies. Living things are generally repulsed by us, our composition.

My cock was incredibly hard, stiffly sticking out from my body like a post, and Travis's ass was spread out before me, soft and willing, his asshole exquisitely stretched around my fingers. "Go ahead and slide it in there," Travis said, breathless. "Dad can take it."

Sex is important. It's how we connect. With each other, it strengthens our familial bond, gives us strength and protection. And it's one way we have of connecting with humans, with understanding them. Knowing them as individuals makes them so much more edifying when it's time to consume them.

45

I positioned myself behind him and pressed my hard cock to his asshole. It was slick and lubed up—self-lubing was a trait he'd developed over the years, his asshole no more a human asshole than any other part of his body. I felt his hole kiss the head, wanting to draw me in, but I was so hard that my cock popped right back up. We readjusted, Travis moved his ass downward a little, lining his hole up with my cock head. I pushed forward and the head sank inside.

"Oh, fuck," Travis moaned. His asshole spasmed around my cock and I thought I'd cum but I let it rest, regained my bearings. He held a hand to my abdomen to keep me from pushing forward, to adjust himself. My breath synced with his and slowly, imperceptibly, I inched inside him, seeming to do it without even pushing, him drawing me inward.

It felt like heaven. The image of the cavern just off to the room came into my head, the dirt walls of it moving, embracing me, wrapping me up in them and pushing me down the hall to what?

Finally my balls were pressed against his ass and he let out a deep breath. I fell onto his back. My hands went to his neck and he brought them to his face. He kissed my finger, nibbled it, and I felt his teeth.

Proto fangs. Just sharp enough to where I could feel that they weren't … normal. "Fuck me," he said. My slight blond bush of pubes was pressed to the brush of dark hair around his asshole. I licked the back of his neck. Found his jugular vein, pulsing, and licked it, feeling the power of it, charging blood through his system. Blood that both was his and wasn't, the flow of it rushing like an underwater rip tide.

I pulled back, let my cock slide out, then pushed it back in. "Fuck yeah, son. Work Dad's ass. Fuck me." Travis's firm cheeks bounced as I pounded my hips against them. I never would have imagined myself fucking this butch older guy, but really the pleasure all seemed to be his. I went slow to keep myself from cumming, but a few times I paused and Travis fucked his ass back onto my cock like he couldn't stop taking it. I would feel the cum rise up in my nuts, but he always knew exactly when to rest and let me get control again.

It was only after he began to lift himself off the couch and I slid out of him, allowed him to rise, that I saw his face had begun to change. It wasn't so much inhuman was it was swelled and exaggerated, over-ripe. His whole body was puffed up—still slender, but it was like muscles had grown where there hadn't been muscles before, where there shouldn't have been muscles at all. He pushed down on my shoulders, positioned me seated on the sofa, and straddled my lap.

He took hold of my cock with one hand and sat right down on it. Grabbing the back of the couch with one hand and my neck with the other, he fucked himself on my cock in even, fluid motions, my cock going deep into the heart of him each time. He went faster and faster, went into some other state of being, his body getting more and more swelled, hairy angry chest near to bursting. He wasn't smiling but his mouth began to open, and now his fangs were fangs and he was looking into my eyes and I was so close to losing it, to cumming. His pace was insistent, this gorgeous guy—thing—taking me but let-ting me take him, the dominant and submissive intertwined, victim and killer, one and the same. My nuts crept up into my body and the fear I felt ran side by side with lust and made me feel crazed, unhinged.

He brought his face closer to mine, closer to my neck. Those fangs …

"I'm gonna cum," I said, thinking *I'm afraid and I don't know if I …*

His eyes became yellow and translucent as he fucked himself on my cock and licked my neck, just a swipe of his tongue right along my vein. I felt the cum rise up in my nuts and then he slammed his ass down onto me and I was past the point of no return. He stayed still as my cock swelled and shot the first jet of cum into him. Just as it did, he sank his fangs into my neck.

They were thin as needles at the tips but thickened from there, and I felt every centimeter of them as they pierced into me, widening two holes into my skin, popping the thick wall of my vein.

He began to suck. The power of it was surprising. The life began to drain out of me instantly, all of this happening in one moment, my cock still shooting into him, my seed and my blood draining into him at the same time—me into him, him from me, a closed circuit. Pleasure flooding my body still even as my life flowed out of it. *This is it,* I thought, *I could die but I'm not going to, he's going to bring me over, I have to trust him.*

My orgasm subsided as my life began to subside, my heart thudding slower, my vision blurring. Sleep crept up and then walloped me over the head. I was aware that he was still feeding from me, but the torrent of blood that was going into him became more of a trickle. Somehow I could feel the struggle in him to stop, to not just keep going and take it all, to take my life. How easy it would be just to suck a little more, suck up that last delicious morsel of my life, tasty as the last bit of salty pie crust on the plate, swallow it down and let my body float away, having served its purpose.

My vision went dark. I saw myself traveling down that cavern, and now I knew where it led: into the ocean, into an abyss, a place where they sank the bodies, a dark and endless place.

Travis tore himself away. He screamed. His mouth was wide open and dripping black red, my blood drooling down his chin. A total animal now, a demon, but it was all like a dream as my vision contracted further.

I was vaguely aware of him reaching behind himself, pulling out a razor. He slashed it across his wrist and shoved it into my mouth, and the taste …

It hit my tongue with a sizzle, an almost electric shock. I wanted it. That tingle as the first trickle of his blood (my blood—and the blood of all he'd ever killed) went down my throat. It was the most delicious thing I'd ever tasted and I locked my mouth to his arm like a leech, sucking messily, greedily. No thought in my head but the intense want of it. I bit down and my blunt teeth tore open the flesh of his arm, making even more of a mess, blood all over my face and dripping down my neck, chest, abdomen, to my cock, which was still inside of him, still hard.

Blood filled me, and as it did my vision got clearer, like I was swimming upward to the surface of the water. Then I *broke* the surface, and in a flash I was soaring above it, roaring right up into the dark sky and looking down at myself. The room in the cave was as clear as if it were in four dimensions, a shift as swift and violent as the shock wave from a nuke which blasted through my body, pain and exhilaration one and the same. My head felt like it was pressed in a vice and split open like a watermelon. I screamed.

Undead. I'd come over. Pain like I never felt, but it began to subside as my cock slipped out of Travis's ass. I was still in space, still looking down, the earth laid out for me like a satellite map, you zoom in and see the tiniest speck of sand, so clear you could count each one. And there was Travis, his whole body now unswelled, back to normal. But he didn't look like he used to. Nothing did. I was seeing it all for the first time.

He was seeing me for the first time.

"Welcome," he said.

MY VAMPIRE GURU

Gerard Wozek

The trouble with listening to the meditation downloads at night was that Najam's deep voice was mesmerizing. Once I started listening to his soft, gentle tones in bed, I would quickly drift off to sleep and have the most erotic fantasies one could imagine. The dreams were so lucid, in fact, that the first few times they occurred, I was convinced they had genuinely happened.

I remember waking up several times drenched in sweat, with sticky pre-cum smeared across my disheveled boxer shorts. Both my neck and underarms felt wet with a saliva-like substance, as if someone had brusquely rubbed their stubbly beard across them, leaving my skin bruised, nearly broken open, and tender to the touch. Even the headphones I had placed snugly over my ears had somehow been removed from my head and tossed to the other side of my mattress.

Had I taken them off in my sleep? Had I actually dreamt these strange and sexy encounters, or did they really happen?

Najam's creative visualizations were online and free to download at first. I stumbled upon his work while looking for some alternative and holistically-minded ways to relax. One click on an advertisement and I found myself engaged in somewhat esoteric reading material from a man who positioned himself somewhere between an authentic living saint and a new age self-help guru from New Delhi.

The more I read his philosophy on living and listened to the strangely seductive tracks from his Web site, the more I became enamored of Najam. He was older, with flecks of soft gray in his thick black hair, but he appeared almost ageless. There was a youthful twinkle that danced out of his piercing dark eyes—eyes that seemed to follow me from every picture. They were definitely the main attraction, offsetting his placid, handsome face.

Najam's masculine countenance was dark, rugged, and steady, with a mustached smile that sent me on numerous online image searches to find more pictures of him. In fact, I found myself using his face as wallpaper on my laptop and would often stop what I was doing jsut to gaze at the photograph, lapsing into distracted moments as I looked longingly into his mysterious eyes.

"Men, you must surrender to the understanding that your virility is boundless," Najam proclaimed in a heavy accent in his video ad. "Download my new sensuality series and your sexual life will transform. My intense visualizations will enhance your masculine vibrancy and open up new worlds for you."

How could I resist? So what if most of the chanting over a sitar was indecipherable? What did it matter that a good portion of Najam's lectures were in a language that was completely foreign to me? I could catch a few familiar words and phrases—*believe in your eternal nature, surrender to the ultimate power, fondle, ejaculate, ecstatic longing*—that fell in between the other words in Hindi.

But what really mattered was that the words were emanating from him. Warmly familiar, subtly erotic, his deep, heavy intonations were a cross between Barry White and Deepak Chopra. I had a sense at times that his voice was inside me, that Najam himself was cradled inside me—haunting me, possessing me. Always within a few minutes of listening, I felt as if I were under a heady and somewhat poisonous spell.

I typically felt sedated and somewhat eroticized after listening to the lectures. Sometimes before falling asleep, I would take off my pajamas, run a hot shower, and beat off, imagining Najam's beautiful lips on mine. I'd stand with my erect cock in my hand and take long slow strokes while streams of warm water ran down my back and buttocks. I'd close my eyes, imagine his thick arms around my waist, and call out his name until I'd throw back my head and collapse into rapture.

At times I tried listening to Najam in my car while driving to work. But I found myself glazing over and veering off the road a few times. When I played the mantra-like lessons at home, I would find myself in a trance, walking about my apartment in a daze, heading towards the divan or the bedroom to recline, then later perhaps, a masturbation session in the shower.

"At least it's deeply relaxing me," I told myself. "If nothing else, I'm totally at peace when I'm listening to his voice."

And after a while that's all that mattered to me: hearing his soothing voice, settling in to the rhythm of his sentences, and drifting off into another realm.

As time progressed however, I found myself unable to sleep if I didn't have the lecture series playing in my ears. I'd toss and turn in bed and become overheated and restless until I finally gave in. I became accustomed to keeping my iPod under my pillow and reaching for it habitually, just so I could hear his deep voice and fall into a daze, like some potent narcotic I had suddenly become addicted to.

The more I became habituated to the electronic meditations, the more vivid my dreams became. At first, the images were hazy: the outline of a honey glazed chest and broad shoulders, a wide, thrusting torso, the mushroom head of a thick, dark cock, massive and desirable, moving in and out of shadows, just inches in front of me.

Seeing this dark, sexy creature, I was always sliced through with a fierce desire, an intense hunger to be seized by this brooding masculine figure. I would lean my face in closely so that I was right next to his sizeable shaft and bulging testicles. I would often just open my mouth and dangle my tongue, crazed and begging for the engorged penis to cross over my lips and plunge down my throat, but it remained just an inch or so above my chin, taunting me, torturing me, exciting me in a way I never imagined.

For weeks the ghostly visage would visit me but I could never make out anything above the prominent Adam's apple. And as I approached the sexy frame of my headless dream lover, the image would dissolve into smoke, surrounding me in a cloud of vapor that made me tingle and swoon in a way that was completely out of character for me. As the smoke wafted over me, I would drift out of consciousness, though often times I could still feel my rock-hard cock engulfed in a warm, womb-like mouth. I would very often open my eyes, suddenly alone, prone on my mattress, still thrusting into the bed sheets, grasping my spurting wet shaft with my fist.

Time and time again, I tried to look up and see the face of my mysterious visitor or attempt to touch and feel the man who appeared before me. But it was useless. I was a prisoner to my unrequited desire. I was completely and utterly engaged with a voice, a fantasy man who was becoming so real to me in dreams that it began to frighten me.

"Use me as you wish," I would often plead to my ominous master in these ongoing dreams. "Take me as your slave. I'll obey your commands, do whatever you want."

I was months into Najam's sensuality series and using my credit card to download more programs. Curious to know where the next lecture would take me, I couldn't seem to satiate my need to hear more of this hypnotic philosopher's musk-infused meditations. I thought that at some point, if I kept listening, I would finally have the dream and get to see the face of the charismatic stranger.

"If it's you, Najam," I cried out one night before putting on the headphones, "If you are really the one, my one and only guru, my dream lover, then show yourself. I want to kiss you and never stop."

And with that impassioned plea, it happened.

My first recollection was that my head was ensconced, not between the ear pads of my headphones, but between two massively toned thighs. I was gently being rocked back and forth, to and fro, in a hot sandwich of oiled masculine muscle. I reached up and could finally feel the strength of my lover's two powerful legs, and reaching further upward, I embraced and began kneading his massively strong and musky buttocks.

My tongue instinctively began to wag between his scrotum and dangling balls as I slowly worked my way up to and around the giant shaft that was fully erect and waiting for my needy mouth. I indulged in deep sucking, almost cumming myself when my lips first tasted the salty semen on the tip of his fat head. It was an elixir to me. I moved my head back and forth along his wet cock as though it were the only reason for being.

I stopped momentarily to gaze up at the smooth, chiseled chest and the moist olive tinged nipple darts hanging down. I rose slowly and took my time gently sucking and tasting each one. Then I stood up and kissed the stubble on the wide neck of my lover. Yes, I could see the taut nape of his neck, his broad chin, and yes, yes, finally his mouth. It was indeed those perfect soft lips framed by that dark moustache I had come to hope for. It was unmistakably Najam!

I closed my eyes and let my lips touch his, too frightened to take in the eyes of my master, let alone the entire handsome face. We kissed the electric kiss. Our mouths gently opened and our tongues began their hungry search over and over each other. Then, after what seemed to be nearly an hour or so of hungry, passionate face mashing, he gently pulled his mouth away from me and firmly turned me around so that my back and naked buttocks were facing him.

There was no warning for what happened next. No gentle probing of his tongue in my ass, no fingering of my wet hole or massaging of my sphincter with lube, just a sudden animal-like mounting with his knees around my waist and a fast and momentous seizure of ecstasy.

I let out a shocked cry of both terror and pleasure as he rammed his warm and stiff manhood into my opening. He held me solidly from behind and pushed deeper and further into me until my spread cheeks were plum with his torso.

I was captive. Feeling my own rock-hard cock and trying to keep myself from exploding into bliss, I focused on his heavy breathing and the now familiar elongated syllables I had come to appreciate through those downloads for so many months.

"Fuck me, master Najam," I cried out as I felt my cock stiffening into the place of no return. "I need you so badly, take me."

His breath became more rapid. His crazed thrusting from behind accelerated and became more animated. He wrapped his thick arms around my chest as I had longed for and brought his mouth down to inhale my neck. With each crazed push inside of me, his nape sucking became more intense.

"Go ahead and leave your love mark," I whispered to the mad sex fiend whose eyes I still had not gazed into. And as he bit down into my flesh with fiery passion, the ominous thread of moaning became louder. As I screamed with pleasure, I came into a new awareness.

I was suddenly in my bed, alone, shaken, and exhausted from being so violently manhandled. I collapsed into a cold sweat, naked and terrified and in a state of complete bewilderment.

What just happened? Where had my ultimate lover gone? How could this be real? How could dreams be so visceral?

For days after, I could barely walk. It was as though I had been seized by some kind of flu-like fatigue. I was drained and pale and without an appetite. I couldn't work, couldn't eat, and could hardly find the strength to even listen to Najam's resonant voice, which astonished me because I had become so accustomed to falling asleep to his consonants and vowels.

My neck showed no visible signs of a love hickey or dark bruising, but when I touched the area where his mouth had been, I felt a painful ache. I languished in this kind of hazy stupor for days, drinking water, taking toast when I could hold it down, and browsing the Internet in search of a cause for my symptoms, a remedy for this inexplicable malaise.

It was while I was searching a health board on mononucleosis that I wondered if there were any online discussion boards on the teachings of Najam. Why hadn't I thought of this before? Had I been so caught up in this charismatic leader's presence that I hadn't done any objective investigative background checks?

There were more than a dozen fan sites devoted to the enigma that was Najam. Accolades and endorsements came from a number of established writers, philosophers, and modern new age advocates, all of whom were apparently quite well known in India, but none who were the least bit familiar to me.

As I searched deeper, what I found startled and shocked me. There was a discussion thread on the "psychic vampirism also known as Najam."

The discussion board, titled Najam, The Vampire Guru, underlined the idea that there is a way one can be controlled by an individual who feeds off one's life force—or, as they labeled it in the online thread, one's "prana." Often times they are cult leaders, like Najam.

The site repeated terms like *energy vampire, energy predator, energy parasite,* and *pranic vampire* as it referenced the man whose face I had wallpapered on my laptop.

"He gets inside your dreams, only seeking willing, often overly trusting males," one member of the thread declared. "He is a master at using sex talk and the sensual arts to connive and control his victims, draining them of their will to live, until they submit their entire livelihood to his cult."

One thread member who called himself "Cadeucesbearer" insisted that "Najam is a hostile and wicked paranormal entity. He lives off the energy of men who succumb to his seductive voice. He is what is known in Hindu folklore as a "vetala"—a flesh eater or blood drinker, trapped in a zone somewhere between death and the afterlife. Never look into his eyes or he will have you as his victim."

"He will have you," I repeated out loud to myself. And then suddenly from some place inside of me, from some life force that still remained deep within my core, I declared. "He will *not* have me."

As I read further, the writer offered advice on breaking the bond: "According to sacred Hindu texts, the person can get rid of a vetala's hold by chanting a mantra: 'Durgamba durgamba durgaa durgae durgamba, Om namaha Shivaya,' which means 'Mother and father of the universe please rescue me.' Do this in the vetala's presence and you will be free."

In the days that followed, I did my best to detox from the suffocating and darkly sinister influence of Najam. But just deleting the programs from my laptop and other devices wasn't sufficient—they kept popping back up. And Najam's Web site, which appeared to be gone from the cache, would suddenly come up in a random search.

It was clear to me that my computer and electronic devices were deeply infected. A worm had found its way into my digital life and I was determined to extricate the virus completely. Rather than find a computer exorcist, I decided to simply dispose of my computer, trade in my music device for a new one, and even give away my old headphones. I wanted no remaining remnants of Najam.

But switching out my equipment and electronics was just part of it—I had to get the insidious worm out of my psyche as well. At first I resisted sleeping. I would stay up for most of the night, reading books or taking showers, jerking off until I'd fall into an exhausted, dreamless heap. Then I'd stumble off to work and take quick naps in my car.

After a few weeks of this routine, I felt safe from the influence of Najam. For extra protection and safety, I decided to wear a small locket around my neck with the spell-breaking mantra written on a sheet of paper and folded inside of it. But I was able to return to bed at a normal hour, without the need to listen to the master's voice. The first few days I slept without incident, but on the fifth night I was once again seized by that nearly inaudible hum. It was like a faraway moaning, a sad, mournful cry that was both sexual and full of impossible torment at the same time.

I tossed around in my bed for hours until I lost consciousness. It was then that I was visited once again by the mesmerizing and imposing figure.

I was suddenly aware again that I was kneeling on my bed before the dark master, my head flush with his large, imposing feet. Instinctively I began to lick his toes and gingerly kiss his ankles. I felt both terror and desire for him at the same time. How could I be so inextricably drawn to a being that was so loving and so utterly toxic at the same time?

Wild thoughts ran through my mind: Could I make love to him but then be free of his spell? I was weak with desire for him. I still wanted him to fuck me uncontrollably like before. I then thought if I allowed myself to look for the first time at his face, to lie on my back and be mounted by him missionary style while I gazed into his eyes, perhaps it would be all right. Perhaps everything that was written about his vampiric nature was all a lie to distract me from consummating this passionate moment.

I worked my way up his strong hairy legs, stopping for a few moments at his rock-hard cock. I kissed the dark bulbous head, placed my wet lips over his thick shaft, and then buried my nose in his bushy pubic hair. I inhaled his musky scent and let myself linger there for a few moments before licking the delicate trail of black hair that led up to his navel.

I kissed his tight pectoral muscles, smelling the warm scent of jasmine oil there. I began to swoon. My own stiff cock was dripping cum and I fought the desire not to touch myself, needing this sweet and terrifying encounter to last for as long as I could manage.

I licked and gently sucked his two dark nipples until each point was firm and sharply erect, then moved upwards to his taut pectorals, all the while gyrating and mashing my slippery cock over his. Finally I brought my mouth to his neck, where I stopped to kiss his cleft chin with my eyes tightly shut.

"Look at me," my master spoke. "See how much I need you."

I started to tremble uncontrollably. My heart was thumping and I wanted so badly to open my eyes and be taken over by him. He grasped my ass firmly and made a fist of soft backside flesh, pushing me closer to his solid and imposing frame.

For a moment, I felt an unmanageable desire to unite with him, to simply surrender. I wanted to be on my back, my legs spread open, allowing his long pole to pump me wildly like a dog—only this time he would be on top as I willingly gave up my entire soul through my wide-open blue eyes.

A thin layer of indiscernible moaning once again invaded the room—a long thread of ecstatic cries and whispers that seemed to come from nowhere, but served to disorient and knock me off balance. Were these the pleading wails from his other victims?

I stumbled for a moment, dizzy for a breath, letting my mouth graze his mustache and latch onto his waiting tongue. We kissed deeply. Our mouths instinctively united. I let my eyes run over his ears and through his thick, curly hair.

At this moment, I felt a fire within myself that I never knew existed. But it wasn't a flame that called out for me to let go and surrender—it was a blood born blaze of survival.

From this heat inside of me, I discovered some brave, almost superhuman muscular strength there, which allowed me to wrestle him down, turn him over, and shove his face into the mattress below us.

"I see you now," I shouted to my nefarious teacher. "I really see you for what you are."

It was all a matter of seconds. I plunged my unsheathed cock into his wide, hairy ass. He yelled something to me in another language but I persisted. He squirmed and tried to turn over, but I anchored myself around his hips and pushed deeper into his dark, puckered hole.

With one hand, I pushed the back of his head down so that his face went deeper into the pillows and disheveled sheets. With my other hand, I opened the special locket that was hitting my breastbone. And with each thrust into my prone and disabled guru, I read the mantra that had been safely secured around my neck.

"Durgamba durgamba durgaa durgae durgamba," I said, plunging deeply into his moist crevice, "Om namaha Shivaya!"

Over and over I shouted the prayer, thrusting and sweating and pushing and groaning into him, until the firm muscular flesh became a soft cloud and at last I was only dry fucking my crumpled bed sheets.

I opened my eyes finally and let out a loud gasp. Had I broken the spell? Had I ended this monster's insidious grip on me?

Najam had vanished into damp vapor. I turned over on my back and held my sweat-drenched pillow. For a long time I laid there on the crushed sheets and thought of his mind-blowing body, his sexy, curvy mustached mouth and the way he had taken me from behind that one time, so violently and yet so assuredly. We had been one, my vampire guru and I, but in that instant I was free. The dreams ended, the moaning ceased, the unending malaise lifted, and the craving to hear his voice was gone.

When I closed my eyes the next evening, I imagined a different kind of flesh and blood lover. Someone with kind eyes, someone gentle and warm. Not a master, but an equal; not a teacher, but a companion.

I made up my own incantation to relax, my own personal mantra. "Find me love," I called out to the universe. "Find me here in real waking time."

I fell asleep that night, listening to my own soothing voice, and I slept deeply and soundly. Completely safe.

MOON DOGGIE AND THE NIGHTSURFERS AT HAMMERHEAD BEACH

Michael Bracken

Hammerhead Beach, the site of the bitchinest waves in the northern hemisphere and home to a particularly ravenous population of sharks, had been off-limits to the general public for more than half a century. Most days the beach remained deserted until sunset, when the nightsurfers and the moonbathers arrived. Pale-skinned and cold-blooded, they didn't fear the sharks any more than the sharks feared them, and the two groups had co-existed peacefully for several decades.

Moon Doggie, the first nightsurfer to discover the once-remote beach, had come of age in the sixties, lusting after Frankie Avalon and not Annette Funicello, a time when few surfers dared come out of the Tiki Hut for fear of being shunned as a wooly woofter. Late one night at San Onofre, he and Butch Peterson—a middle-aged surfer who only visited the ocean at night—had wandered far from the bonfire where other surfers and their wahines were drinking beer and dancing barefoot to the music of Dick Dale. Moon Doggie had not returned to the bonfire that night and the next morning realized he'd developed an aversion to sunlight and a taste for blood.

He spent the next year with Peterson until the older nightsurfer's board smashed against a reef at Teahupoo on the southwest tip of Tahiti, breaking apart and sending a thick stake of balsa through his heart. Without Peterson's continued guidance, Moon Doggie learned to fend for himself in his new state of existence, forever twenty-three and still in search of the perfect wave.

The beach parties had changed just as Moon Doggie had changed. The nightsurfers and moonbathers built no bonfires, for they needed neither the heat nor the light, and their only music was the sound of the waves racing to the shore.

Moon Doggie surveyed the moonbathers in their baggies and string bikinis as he carried his big gun across the sand and into the water. Like his, their skin was so pale it was nearly translucent, and because it reflected moonlight rather than absorbed it, they glowed with a faint luminescence.

After he strapped his leash to his ankle, Moon Doggie paddled out to where two other nightsurfers waited, but they didn't speak. Each remained attentive to the feel of the ocean waiting for the perfect wave to break, and Moon Doggie took his turn when it came.

After three hours of hot-dogging, Moon Doggie returned to the shore, lay down on his beach towel, and closed his eyes. He didn't sleep—that was reserved for daylight hours—but he did relax. For a time. Twenty minutes after he lay down, Moon Doggie's eyes snapped open and he rose on one elbow. The wind had shifted, and he smelled blood and testosterone.

He turned upwind and narrowed his eyes, trying to find the source. Around him, other nightsurfers and moonbathers did the same. He pulled on his huarache sandals, stood, and began walking north along the beach, following the scent. When one of the other nightsurfers rose and began to follow, Moon Doggie turned and glared, his gaze burning with an intensity that was no mere reflection of moonlight. The other nightsurfer, a recent convert still learning the hierarchy of the beach, hesitated and glanced around. When he saw that none of the others had risen to follow the scent, he returned to his blanket.

Satisfied that he remained the Big Kahuna and would not again be challenged, Moon Doggie walked alone along the sandy beach until it ended at a rocky outcropping fifty feet high that bisected the sand and jutted into the ocean. He climbed and, after he crested the outcropping, looked down at a cove below where a pair of dick draggers— boogie boarders—were drinking wine from a box and fondling each other next to a roaring bonfire. They only had eyes for one another and could not see much beyond the circle of light cast by their fire.

The two twentysomething dick draggers reclined on a blanket, their board shorts already discarded and their boogie boards forgotten. Their bodies were taut but not overtly muscular, their skin bronzed, and their hair sun-bleached blond and blonder. Tyler lifted the wine box above Wayne's face and twisted the spigot handle until a thin stream of red wine trickled out. Wayne gulped down one mouthful and then another, but just as much wine stained his Vandyke and dribbled down to the blanket below his head as he actually swallowed. After several gulps, he pushed the box away and Tyler twisted the spigot closed.

Tyler tossed the wine box aside, leaned forward, and kissed Wayne. He sucked wine from the other man's facial hair before kissing his way down Wayne's neck, chest, and abdomen to the closely cropped triangle of auburn hair nesting Wayne's ball sac and erect cock. He reached between Wayne's thighs and cupped his balls as he took the head of Wayne's cock between his lips. He licked away the glistening drop of pre-cum that crowned it and slowly took the entire length of cock into his mouth. A moment later he drew back until his teeth caught on the other man's glans. Then he did it again.

The two boogie boarders had been flirting for several weeks, letting each other know of their mutual interest, but their evening visit to the beach had been Tyler's idea. He'd packed hot dogs, chips, wine, matches, and a new tube of lube. They'd brought their boogie boards—their pretext for visiting the beach though neither of them had actually intended to enter the water. Tyler had managed to light a driftwood bonfire but they hadn't even opened the package of hot dogs. Instead, they had spent much of the time since their arrival drinking wine and making out. Their board shorts had been discarded a scant few minutes before Moon Doggie crested the outcropping and stared down at them, and Tyler finally had Wayne exactly the way he'd dreamed him about during all those weeks of flirting.

As he continued his oral manipulation of Wayne's cock, Tyler massaged Wayne's balls and stroked the sensitive spot behind them with the tip of his finger. When Wayne's cock began to stiffen, his hips began to move, and he reached down to thread his fingers in Tyler's hair, Tyler knew the other man couldn't restrain himself much longer.

Tyler sucked Wayne's cock deep into his mouth until the mushroom cap pressed against the back of his throat. As the same time he pressed the tip of his finger against the tight pucker of Wayne's asshole and pressed. As Wayne's ass opened to accept Tyler's finger, he came.

Though Tyler swallowed and swallowed again, he couldn't swallow fast enough and a potent mixture of his saliva and Wayne's cum slid down the length of Wayne's shaft into his lap where it clung to his pubic hair.

Tyler slowly withdrew his finger but didn't release his oral hold on Wayne's cock until he had licked it clean.

The intoxicating mix of scents—blood, testosterone, cum, wine, and burning driftwood—rose from the cove to tingle Moon Doggie's nostrils. He wet his cold lips with the tip of his tongue and felt the needle-sharp points of his canines as he watched the two young men on the beach below. He sported a woody and his erection strained against his baggies, demanding release. Torn between his desire to feed and his desire to fuck, Moon Doggie continued his silent vigil until the two dick draggers finally kicked sand over the burning embers of their fire and gathered their things.

By the time Moon Doggie returned to Hammerhead Beach, most of the other nightsurfers and moonbathers had gone. He grabbed his beach towel and big gun and carried them to his psychedelically painted Volkswagen panel van. After securing the surfboard to the roof rack, he drove several miles inland to the two-bedroom home he'd purchased several years earlier, and closed the automatic garage door only moments before the first light of dawn found his neighborhood. He hurried through the house to the windowless basement where he would spend much of his day sleeping before going out that evening to feed.

Tyler crawled out of bed early that evening, showered, and dressed for work at Tommy's Tiki Hut, a faux Polynesian bar where butt crumbs, waxboys, and gapers went to impress and hit on tourists staying at the nearby hotels. Unless employed by Tommy, few real surfers ever entered the Hut.

Before leaving home, Tyler sent Wayne a text about their evening together and was surprised when he hadn't received a response by the time he reached work. Midnight came and went, as did several of the romance writers and the faux surfers they invited back to their hotel rooms, before Tyler had a chance to look at his cell phone again. Wayne still hadn't responded, so Tyler sent him another message, this one an explicit description of what he would do the next time they were together.

Tyler checked his phone again at the end of his shift and still hadn't received a reply from Wayne. Wayne also didn't respond to the next dozen texts he sent or return any of Tyler's phone calls. Three days after their carnal encounter on the beach, increasingly pissed that Wayne had used him and then put the slow fade on him, Tyler was ripe for Moon Doggie's mid-week midnight approach at Tommy's Tiki Hut.

The bar was quiet that night, with few tourists and none of the usual contingent of butt crumbs, waxboys, and gapers ready to hit on them, and Moon Doggie straddled a stool at the end of the bar nearest the exit. Though he still felt a little sluggish from his last feeding, he had another craving to satisfy.

Tommy's Tiki Hut specialized in umbrella drinks, but after taking Moon Doggie's order Tyler filled a mug with the cheap beer on tap and slid it across the bar to the nightsurfer.

Except for pale skin that made Moon Doggie look like a cavefish, he had the look of a surfer, so Tyler said, "I haven't seen you in here before."

"I saw you on the beach the other night with your friend," he said. "I wanted to meet you."

Tyler had only visited the beach at night once in the previous several months so he knew exactly which night Moon Doggie meant. He said, "Wayne's no friend. I thought we had something, but that bitch used me and dumped me."

"That's a shame." Moon Doggie reached across the counter and took Tyler's hand in his. "You deserve better."

Tyler felt an unexpectedly cool tingle shoot through his body and his cock hardened. For the first time he looked into Moon Doggie's eyes and was mesmerized.

Moon Doggie said, in a seductive whisper, "I want you."

Tyler swallowed hard. "I get off at two."

Moon Doggie released his hold on Tyler's hand, breaking the spell, and slipped off the stool. He tossed a crumpled five-dollar bill on the bar but it wasn't until a few minutes after the door closed behind him that Tyler realized the nightsurfer hadn't touched the beer.

The last two hours of Tyler's shift crawled past, and he rushed through the back door as soon as he clocked out. Moon Doggie waited there, leaning against his van, and through the open door Tyler saw the mattress covering the Volkswagen's floor. Any other time he would have thought twice about climbing into the van of someone he had met only hours earlier, but something about Moon Doggie made him difficult to resist.

Moon Doggie climbed in after Tyler, closed the door, and sat cross-legged on the mattress facing his nervous guest. Black curtains covered the rear windows and another separated the front seats from the rest of the van, effectively cocooning them in darkness. Moon Doggie had inherited the van from Peterson and the curtains were only a small part of what Peterson had done to make the rear area completely light safe. They had spent many months sleeping in the van prior to Peterson's fatal encounter with a splintered surfboard, and Moon Doggie had spent several more until he purchased his house with its windowless basement.

Though Moon Doggie could see in the darkness, he knew Tyler could not. To provide light for his guest, he lit a string of tiny white LED Christmas tree lights that were strung around the inside of the van, and then turned and stared into the nervous boogie boarder's eyes. He touched his middle finger just below Tyler's ear and traced the jaw line to his chin, lifting Tyler's face ever so slightly as he did. Then he pressed his lips against the young man's, feeling the warmth of Tyler's breath on his cheek as the boogie boarder relaxed and slowly exhaled.

Tyler's lips parted as Moon Doggie's kiss grew more insistent, and the nightsurfer thrust his tongue into the young man's mouth, feeling the heat of Tyler's oral cavity envelope it. The kiss was deep and hard and unintentionally stole the younger man's breath until Tyler pulled away.

As Tyler struggled to breathe, Moon Doggie unbuttoned the blue Hawaiian shirt Tyler wore for work, pushed it open, and rested his palm flat against the boogie boarder's chest to feel the young heart beating beneath the ribs. A moment later he pushed the shirt from Tyler's shoulders and let it slide down the young man's sun-bronzed arms. Then the tip of his tongue followed the path his finger had earlier, down Tyler's jawline from his ear to his chin. Instead of traveling upward to the young man's lips, though, he continued drawing a wet line down Tyler's neck. He let the tip of his tongue linger on Tyler's jugular vein, feeling the hot blood pulse beneath the skin. Had he not still been satiated by his most recent feeding, Moon Doggie would have been tempted to sink his teeth into the boogie boarder's vein and slowly draw out the young man's life force.

He resisted the temptation and drew his tongue down Tyler's hairless chest until he could suck one erect nipple between his teeth. He gently nipped it, not hard enough to draw blood but hard enough for the pain to cause Tyler to pull away. As he did, Moon Doggie pushed Tyler back on the mattress, grabbed his loose-fitting cargo shorts and boxers and jerked them down the younger man's legs to his knees, exposing his erect cock. When Tyler lifted his legs, Moon Doggie removed the young man's huarache sandals, pants, and boxers and tossed them toward the rear of the van.

Unlike Wayne, Tyler was a natural blond, not a sun-bleached blond with contrary evidence concealed beneath his shorts, and his cock rose firm and erect from the tangled nest at the juncture of his thighs. Moon Doggie wrapped one fist around Tyler's erection,

69

thumbed the mushroom cap several times, and then released his grip. He stuck the ball of his thumb in his mouth and tasted the glistening bit of pre-cum that he'd wiped from the tip of Tyler's cock head.

Then he dove forward, almost ravenous in his desire, and took the entire length of Tyler's cock into his mouth, surprising the young man. Blond pubic hair tickled his nose until he drew back and caught the back of his teeth on the boogie boarder's swollen glans.

The young man's hips began to buck up and down as he thrust himself upward to meet Moon Doggie's face each time it descended into his lap. The nightsurfer could feel the increasing tension in the young man's hips and the way his cock strained against his lips, and he was prepared when Tyler finally erupted inside his mouth.

Just as the young man came, Moon Doggie pricked his dorsal artery with the tip of one tooth and drew a thin stream of oxygenated blood into his mouth to mix with the young man's wad of warm cum, and he swallowed everything easily.

When Tyler's cock stopped spasming in his mouth, Moon Doggie drew back, releasing his oral grip on the young man's member. As he did, the tiny wound from which he had drawn Tyler's blood immediately sealed shut.

Moon Doggie's own cock was hard by then, straining for release, and Tyler didn't resist when Moon Doggie flipped the younger man onto his stomach, grabbed his waist, and pulled him up onto his knees. He grabbed a half-used tube of lube from a pocket on the van door and slathered it into Tyler's ass crack before positioning himself behind him. He pressed the head of his cock against the younger man's lube-slickened sphincter, grabbed Tyler's hips, and then pushed forward. The boogie boarder opened to accommodate him and soon Moon Doggie buried his entire length in the younger man's ass.

He held Tyler's hips as he drew back and pushed forward, fucking the younger man so hard and so fast that the van—even with its specially reinforced suspension system—rocked back and forth. Years had passed since Moon Doggie last took a lover, and despite his other powers, he could not hold back. He came and came hard, firing cool cum deep into Tyler's ass, and he held the boogie boarder's cheeks tight against his crotch until his cock ran dry.

Then he pulled back, spun the younger man onto his back and stared into his eyes.

When Tyler awoke in his own bed that afternoon he didn't remember when he'd stepped out of the pale surfer's van, didn't remember the drive home, and didn't remember slipping into his own bed. He did remember the sex and he did remember the way the other man had stared into his eyes.

When he pulled open the curtains, he was surprised by how bright the afternoon sun seemed and quickly pulled them closed. Though he didn't noticed the tiny scab on the underside of his cock where Moon Doggie had sampled his blood as part of a blood-sperm cocktail, he was already experiencing the effects of the nightsurfer's bite.

Tyler remained inside with the curtains closed until it was time for work, and he went through the motions that night without paying much attention to the tourists who settled in at the bar and tried to capture his attention. He didn't perk up until he found Moon Doggie's van parked outside the rear door of Tommy's Tiki Hut when he left work at two a.m.

For the next few hours—and for the next few mornings—they continued their carnal exploration of one another's bodies, and each time Moon Doggie drew just a tiny bit of Tyler's blood, the wound sealing closed as soon as he withdrew the tip of his canine tooth. At home, Tyler stopped opening his curtains, and on the third night didn't even bother cooking the hamburger meat he'd purchased for dinner.

He blamed the hours spent in Moon Doggie's van for his increasing lethargy, but didn't understand why his eyes hurt in even dim sunlight and why he'd developed a taste for steak tartare.

Moon Doggie suggested a visit to the beach for Tyler's first night off from work. He picked the boogie boarder up just after sunset and drove to Hammerhead Beach far south of town.

"I thought no one surfed here," Tyler said as Moon Doggie parked his van behind a line of other vehicles.

"Not everyone is afraid."

Tyler helped Moon Doggie remove the surfboard from the roof of the van, then grabbed their blanket and followed him down to the beach where several nightsurfers and moonbathers had already laid claim to their patches of sand. Unlike every other beach party Tyler had attended, there were no fires and there was no music, only moonlight and the sound of the waves breaking.

The nightsurfers and moonbathers grew restless whenever blood walked among them, and had Tyler accompanied anyone other than Moon Doggie—Hammerhead Beach's Big Kahuna—they might have fallen upon him and torn him asunder. As it was, they just stared as he walked past, making Tyler feel like the Benny he was.

Moon Doggie stopped, had Tyler spread the blanket, and then led him across the beach. After Moon Doggie strapped on his leash, he walked his big gun into the water. When he stood waist deep, he had Tyler climb on the front of the board. Then he climbed on the back and paddled away from the shore, duck diving through a pair of waves until they reached the line-up and he turned the board toward the shore. That's when Tyler saw the first shark fin slicing through the water in the distance.

"They usually leave us alone but they know you're here," Moon Doggie said. He snapped up so that he was standing on the board with Tyler still on his knees before him. "Makes me hard just thinking about it."

The bulge in Moon Doggie's baggies emphasized his point and Tyler reached for it. He stroked Moon Doggie's erection through the wet material until Moon Doggie pushed his hand away and freed his cock by shoving his shorts down. As Tyler moved to take the head of Moon Doggie's cock in his mouth, the nightsurfer shifted his position to keep the board balanced. At the same time, several moonbathers and nightsurfers lined up along the beach like luminescent Maoi statues, staring out at the copulating couple on the surfboard.

Tyler's tongue licked all the way around Moon Doggie's cock, but Moon Doggie wasted no time. He grabbed the back of Tyler's head and shoved his cock all the way into Tyler's oral cavity. He drew back and did it again, face-fucking the younger man hard and fast, oblivious to the ever-increasing number of fins circling the board.

Moon Doggie came hard, erupting within Tyler's mouth, and the younger man could not swallow fast enough to keep the nightsurfer's cum from spilling from the corners of his mouth. He drew back quickly, unbalancing the surfboard beneath them. Moon Doggie reflexively adjusted his position to keep them from spilling into the water.

"We shouldn't be out here," Tyler said, his gaze following the path of a shark fin that passed only a few feet from the board. "It isn't safe."

"If you were one of us you wouldn't fear our brethren."

"One of you what?"

Moon Doggie explained what he and the creatures lining the beach were. Nightsurfers and moonbathers didn't live in castles, turn into bats, or fear garlic-laden Italian food, but they were every bit as much creatures of the night as popular culture and low-budget horror movies made them out to be. When Moon Doggie finished, Tyler understood his recent lethargy, his aversion to sunlight, and his new dietary desires. He had been changing to become one of them, but he had not completed the transition, a transition to which he had to agree before Moon Doggie could finish what he had started that first night in the back of his van.

"Join us and experience an endless summer," Moon Doggie offered. "Or take your chances swimming to shore."

Tyler looked at the dozen shark fins circling them and then toward the nightsurfers and moonbathers on the beach, waiting to finish what the sharks might not. "That isn't much of a choice."

Moon Doggie drew one finger along the boogie boarder's jaw line and smiled. "It's the only one you have."

Tyler looked again at his options and then tilted his head back and to the side, exposing his jugular vein.

Moon Doggie had been sloppy the first few times he'd tried to convert a hot-blooded lover into a cold-blooded nightsurfer, allowing bloodlust to overcome him. He had accidentally drained his lovers' bodies and had been forced to dispose of them in the ocean as shark chum, just as he had disposed of Wayne's body after his most recent feeding.

This time he was careful. He kissed Tyler's neck, felt the warm blood pulsing beneath the younger man's skin, and then pierced Tyler's jugular vein with both of his needle-sharp canine teeth. He carefully drew out the last of Tyler's lifeblood, replacing it with an eternity as a creature of the night.

As Tyler completed his evolution, the moonbathers and night-surfers lined up along the shore returned to their blankets, and the sharks circling Moon Doggie's surfboard drifted away.

A few minutes later, the perfect wave lifted Moon Doggie's big gun, and the two nightsurfers rode it into shore.

IRRESISTIBLE

David Aprys

"You really ought to be showing in Manhattan. Who represents you?" asks the dark-haired man in the bow tie and oversized horn-rimmed glasses.

I grab a champagne flute from a passing waiter with an amazing backside—a real bubble butt. He glances over his shoulder, catches me checking him. We lock eyes and both of us smile. When I take a sip, I fight not to make a face—cheap stuff. Would've expected better bubbly at a gallery opening in the hippest part of Williamsburg. My new admirer moves on, but takes one more backward glance.

"Guy called Larry Birman," I answer while watching Natalia, who runs the gallery, toss her long, hennaed braids and tack a red dot on the wall next to one of my large scale abstract paintings. Another sale—cha-ching.

Grinning, I turn my attention back to Poindexter. "Thing is, I'm thinking of ditching Birman. He takes forty percent and hasn't gotten me anywhere near a Chelsea gallery."

"In that case," he reaches into the breast pocket of his slim-cut suit. "You'll want my card." I turn it over in my hand. Cream colored vellum, embossed navy blue lettering. R. JAMES HIDDLESTON, BROKER/AGENT, it reads, followed by an Upper East Side address.

"Whaddya know? James is my middle name too," I say while scoping for waiter boy. There he is, talking to a couple so-called friends of mine. Better get over there before one moves in for the kill.

"My clients are among the most discerning collectors in New York," says Hiddleston, catching my gaze. "I could do wonders for you."

A truthful boast, or is dude hitting on me? And what's up with the precise way he speaks—is he gunning for dork of the year? Even seems to be faking some kind of British accent.

"You mean work wonders with my career?" I give him a wink. Can't hurt to flirt. He's striking, but not exactly my type. Angular face—wolfish and pale with a prominent nose and a small, secretive slash of red mouth. Might be ten years older than me. But behind those glasses, his eyes—infinite brown velvet—draw me in.

Suddenly, it's way too bright in here. I shield my eyes from the lights glaring against those white, white gallery walls.

"I have many talents." Hiddleston raises an eyebrow. "Suppose we arrange a time next week to discuss your prospects? Have you a regular job?"

"I, uh … work at a bike shop in Bushwick couple days a week, right around the corner from my apartment," I tell him, though not sure why. Like most New Yorkers, I'm wary of strangers.

"Convenient," Hiddleston remarks drily. OK, maybe he *is* good-looking, in an unusual way. "Suppose we meet at my office, two p.m. Tuesday next?"

From behind us comes a crash. Someone has dropped a tray of empty glasses. I only realize how focused I've been on Hiddleston when I break eye contact to look over. It's not my waiter who had the accident, but he's rushing to help. He catches me watching again, gives me a vulnerable smile that says I've got him right where I want him.

Fuck, he's pretty.

"A final incentive," Hiddleston begins. Reluctantly I swing to face him. "Sign with me, and by the end of summer, everyone will know your name and your work will triple in price."

"Next Tuesday at two?" I say, sticking out my hand.

Hiddleston regards my paw as if it's something unclean. Can I help that there's always paint and bike grease under my nails?

His tone is wry as he pats my forearm. "Do make yourself presentable for our meeting, Mr. Lawson. Now, I leave you to your extracurricular activities." With a crisp nod toward my waiter, he turns sharply on his heel and leaves.

My eyes follow him, unsure whether attraction or avarice brings stinging heat to my face. Maybe it's just nerves. For a minute my gut spins, like when I was a kid at the Kanawha County Fair and took one too many rides on the Tilt-A-Whirl.

What's that guy about?

"You staying 'til close?" An inviting voice sounds behind me. "I'm free afterwards."

Hello, waiter boy.

His name is Oscar. A Dominican with caramel brown skin so sweet I can taste it beneath the line of hair that runs from the swirl of his navel to the fragrant thatch between his legs. He's lithe—can't be more than twenty-one. Every inch of his body is tight, like a dancer's. At four in the morning, we tear off each other's clothes while macking in his sliver of a studio apartment. I'm half drunk, giddy with tonight's success and the bump of crystal we did before leaving the local gay bar.

I sway a little, getting to my feet while he slips to his knees, boner peeking from the waistband of his skimpy Andrew Christian briefs.

His tan hands grip my furry thighs while he takes my cock in his mouth. I inhale through my teeth, watching those well-formed lips stretch, allowing entrance to the length of my shaft.

How satisfying, knowing I could've had any of the boys at Metropolitan. But I chose this one—the *other* guy on everyone's radar.

Putting my hands behind my head, I start pumping, gently at first, then not so much. It's so hot, fucking that pretty mouth, watching the kid's eyes widen with admiration as he worships my cock.

He pulls his uncut dick through the fly in his briefs, starts stroking himself. I stare at it, fascinated, and it winks back, moist at the inviting bronze/pink tip. Think I'll have to sample that.

I pull him to his feet and tweak his nipples while kissing him. His hands are all over my hairy chest as he sheds his underwear. I love the little yelp of surprise he makes when I wrap my hand around his dick and thumb the foreskin that barely restrains the sensitive head. I push him to the floor with a rough grunt, positioning my crotch over his face.

He takes me back into his mouth and I feel myself get harder. My tongue flirts with the hooded sheath of his cock as I push it back, savoring the salty, secret taste. I jack him as I lick the length of his dick, deep-throat him.

I know he's getting close, and don't want this to end anytime soon, so I find that soft/hard spot just behind his balls and press my thumb and forefinger to it. A funny giggle escapes from the kid's throat.

"Turn over," I growl. He doesn't need to ask why. Yeah, that ass is perfect. One of the best I've ever seen—and I've seen a few.

Parting his cheeks, I take the barest taste of his hole, stroking his dick from behind. My tongue opens him with wet assurance, getting him ready. Oscar grunts like he's lifting something heavy, tells me he can't wait any longer.

I grab him around the waist, get him on all fours, and lube my thick cock with one hand. Sweat drips from my forehead into my beard and down my chest as I enter him. Oscar cries out, tells me to take it slowly. It's incredible—mastering this smooth-bodied kid who's just starting to put on muscle from working out. I'm brawnier, a bit older, and the contrast—man and boy, leader and follower—gets me closer than I'd intended, and fast.

I thrill to the way he whimpers as I ram myself balls deep into his peachy ass. I pull almost all the way out and shove my cock back in hard, pushing that angelic face into the floor.

There's just enough time to wonder how badly this braided rug is tearing up my knees before I'm cumming, firing spunk into his guts. I don't bother pulling out, it feels too good in there. My sweaty, hardened loins slap his butt while Oscar's wildly hitting his dick. Over his shoulder, I watch him shoot his load all over the floor.

Afterwards, I hold him from behind on the twin bed as he breathes shallowly at first, then deeper. My eyes are already on the door. Just before dawn, I tiptoe through the cluttered room and make my way down five flights of echoing terrazzo stairs.

Walking past Sternberg Park, I'm euphoric. Six of my nine paintings sold before I left the Delray Gallery last night, and I banged the hottest Dominican boy in Brooklyn after celebrating with my besties. Life's pretty damn good.

I spend the weekend working, mostly in the drafty studio I share with four other artists. I've finished my new series of paintings—they're awesome. Sunday afternoon, Oscar texts me while I'm at Bushwick Bikes, chatting up customers. I'll hit him back in a couple days. Don't want him getting the wrong idea.

These kids fall like dominos, I think, smoking a joint in bed Monday morning with a luscious graphic designer. They don't seem to understand that developing a real connection takes time I don't have to give. Call me a taker, but it's not like I pretend to offer anything beyond the immediate.

Tuesday around noon, Natalia from Delray wakes me with an overly chipper phone call. *"Cupio Dissolvi* sold over the weekend." I yawn to hide my excitement. That was the most expensive piece. "Went to a prominent Manhattan collector—a real step up for you. James Hiddleston brokered the deal. Weren't you talking to him at the reception?"

"Shit," I say, glancing at the clock. My stomach knots. "I'm s'posed to meet him at two."

"Mmm …" Natalia sounds like she's thinking. "There's something devious about that nerdy exterior. Be careful. And don't settle for less than sixty percent."

"With his kind of clients," I dodge into my tiny bathroom, stripping off my boxers. "He can have forty percent of me."

"I'm serious, Z." Natalia pauses. "And stay out of his bed—his last playmate was Brian Dottavio. After what happened, Hiddleston ended up with the rights to all his work."

"No worries there." I hang up before she says anything else. Seriously—Brian Dottavio—that's supposed to put me off? The up-and-comer who topped himself last year when he couldn't handle the downtown art scene? Totally had his head up his ass. I'm hungry for money, sex, and recognition. My self-destructive days are in the past.

When I get off the subway, I'm looking pretty snazzy: suede shoes, my best pair of jeans, a plaid shirt and one of those tweed jackets with patches on the elbows. I even scrubbed my fingernails.

I walk through late April fog up to East 71st Street. The address is an exceedingly narrow brownstone—only one window beside the black front door. A dun-colored, four-story Italianate façade. At the ground floor entrance, a gold sign announces the office of R.J.L. Hiddleston.

"Mr. Lawson, delighted to see you." Hiddleston shakes my hand after his assistant shows me into his elegant, minimalist office. "Linnet, please take the afternoon," he says to her. "I'll be occupied with this fine young man."

She gives me a wide-eyed but appraising look as she stalks out on stiletto heels and shuts the door.

Place is a total throwback, looks like the early 1960s in here. I accept a seat in a mid-century modern, straight-backed office chair.

"Sorry to be late," I say. "Guess I owe you my thanks, too. Heard you brokered a deal for one of my paintings in the Delray show." My hand is still tingling where he touched it. The sensation spreads to my whole body.

"Thanks aren't necessary," says Hiddleston, removing his glasses. Must be the overhead lighting that makes him look older than at last Thursday's opening. Would've sworn his hair was all dark then, but today a considerable amount of gray shows. Crow's-feet crease the skin next to his hooded, unknowable eyes. "Your works are extraordinary—such vigorous sensuality in them. One wonders if your personal approach is equally kinetic."

There it is again, a subterranean flash in those watchful brown irises. For a second, I quiver at my core. I try brushing it off as imagination, but a cloud forms over my consciousness.

With a perfectly manicured hand, he slides a folder across his desk. Inside is a contract, several pages long. I flick through it as quickly as my dulled mind allows. Seems pretty standard. Sixty-forty split, I retain full rights over unsold works.

Via text message, I had shitcanned Larry Birman on the way here, so there's nothing to hold me back. Except my better judgment and Natalia's warning.

There's something devious about that nerdy exterior.

"You'll find the terms agreeable," Hiddleston says. Though I'm aware he's modulating his tone to reassure me, it draws me in anyway. "My clients have interest in the unsold pieces at Delray, as well as your past and forthcoming work. You'd be able to quit the unfortunate bicycle shop immediately and concentrate on painting."

I skim the complicated language, past defining words like "property," and "masterwork," and disturbing but unlikely eventualities like "decedent" and "transfer of estate." Then I see the numbers. Enough to pay Manhattan rent for three years. I ink the final page. It's the first time I've seen Hiddleston really smile. It makes him beautiful, arrogant, frightening. Underneath my scrawl, he signs the contract, too.

Upstairs are his intensely masculine private quarters. Again, decorated like the last fifty years never happened. As I fold my jacket over the arm of an Eames sofa, I see it's immaculate. Not a speck of dust on the gleaming wood floor of his study, where he pours three fingers of single malt scotch into antique tumblers. When he hands me one, I notice the scent of his skin—loamy and rich, like the whiskey, or early autumn leaves.

"Shall we seal our agreement?" He suggests, his voice strangely familiar. Our eyes connect with a flame of recognition.

"How do I know you?" I ask, unsure why.

He merely shrugs. "In a sense, you've been waiting for someone like me—someone who really sees you. Aren't you tired of playacting confidence when really, you're as lost as any of the friends you take drugs with, or the young men you so casually use and discard?"

The breath catches in my chest. Suddenly I'm dizzy, and not from the drink. How can he know things about me I've never fully realized?

"Yes, I am," I whisper.

When his fingers touch my skin, my knees begin to tremble. He is slightly taller than me, and his voice fills the room. "Then give yourself to me. And in return, I'll give you a taste of the oblivion you seek."

Where does this feeling come from? God help me, I want to believe this man with nightfall in his gaze.

Then I'm breathing him in, my skin hot beneath his touch. He laughs when, awkwardly, I try to take him in my arms. Instead he folds me into his, teeth mauling the side of my neck hard enough that I know they'll leave a mark.

The man is elegant, but he embraces me with a stevedore's roughness, crushes me against him. Though he appears to have a runner's build, I sense immediately his considerable strength. He could break me in two—like a boy. Like the ones whose calls I don't return because of this inner emptiness.

His dimly lit bedroom is sedate and quixotic. Crisp sheets on the retro-modern four poster bed, wildflowers on the chest of drawers. Beardsley prints on the walls. Windows hung with drapes in myriad shades of beige. Dark wood paneling of the kind only found in old houses.

When I offer him a yielding kiss, Hiddleston pushes me away, shaking his head. It almost comes as a shock. "You artists are all alike," he says, and that slight accent—smooth over vowels and harsh on consonants—comes to prominence. "Mistaking delightful sin for tiresome romance. Take off your bloody clothes."

Maybe I should leave, but I can't. I strip while he watches, silently commanding me. My dick is already standing at attention, though I feel more vulnerable than excited. He pushes me to my knees. His hands, large for a man of his frame, guide the back of my head. My pulse starts to jump.

With greedy fingers, I lower his zipper and reach inside the gray twill trousers. He's hard under my touch, with underwear like nothing I've seen. White flannel, buttoned front. His cock strains against the thin material. I take a tentative lick, but he shakes his head again, and I obey.

83

While I crouch on my haunches, he sheds his shirt and tie, stands over me clad in a snowy white A-shirt. When he nods, I push my hands beneath it, feeling his ridged stomach. With a look of triumph, he pulls the shirt off and tosses it to one side. He keeps his back perfectly straight while removing his underwear.

Unclothed, his body is not like I'd imagined. Beneath the skin, each muscle seems connected by steel tendons. Chiseled and lean, his pale form is a thing of preternatural beauty. It might almost be a Greek statue come to life.

Aside from the ticking clock on the mantelpiece, the only sound I hear is my spellbound, sharp intake of breath.

"Is this what you desire?" He gives me a hard little half-smile.

I'm not sure if he means his cock, jutting towards me like an invitation, or that perfect body. All I can do is shake my head.

Wordlessly, he steps closer. The head of that magnificent tool parts my lips. Already I can't breathe, and it's not really in my mouth. I look up to him for permission. "Carry on," he says as if telling me the time of day.

What happens next is completely unlike the reserve Hiddleston has shown until now, or the smug pragmatism with which I usually approach sex. There are no more words between us. A primal heat arises as I take him into my mouth. I savor every inch of his dick, feel the veins which map its length. It throbs against my tongue, tasting faintly of brine.

He forces it to the back of my throat. A moan rises through his body so powerful I feel it, too. One hand is at the back of my head, pushing until his balls rest on the well-trimmed whiskers of my chin. My eyes and mouth water and I'm choking.

Breathing through my nose, I let it slide out slowly between my lips, twisting my hand around the spit-slicked shaft. It curves upward, nearly as thick at the base as under the glistening head, which I lick like an obscene lollipop.

84

He cradles my face between his cool, perfect hands. Looking down, his eyelids go half mast, engrossed. The corner of his mouth twists with pleasure.

When he moves to a bench at the foot of his bed, I follow, crawling. I've never been subservient to any man, but with this one, who I can't fathom, I would crawl across broken glass. I know that already. The look on Hiddleston's face says he knows it, too.

I crouch between his wide-apart knees, sucking him. One hand works the base of his cock, the other explores the fine black hair on his marble pale legs. A broad triangle of fur runs from groin to navel, where it thins into a silky line that wends its way between his sharply defined abs, and lightly covers the lower part of his chest. With my tongue, I follow this path, chasing a murky, elusive scent.

When I bite gently at his nipples, Hiddleston pulls me by the ears, hard against the flat of his chest. He wants me to savage them, and I do, looking down to see my rigid dick trailing a thread of glistening fluid over his muscular thighs. He flushes warm and pink when I bite harder and grunts his approval, grinding his cock against my flat, furry belly.

Now he wants to kiss me, I can tell before he does it. He stares at me the way cats watch humans, and pulls my head up, crushing my lips to his. How does he taste like honey and darkness at the same time?

This is nothing I've ever felt. My being rocks, his kisses devour. As his tongue ravages my mouth, a strange languor overcomes me. I'm not losing interest—if anything, I'm more turned on than ever. But for the first time, this isn't my game—and I'm not thinking about an exit strategy. What's happening to me? I wonder, as he gathers me in his arms and carries me to the bed as easily if I were driftwood.

His expression is tender, like a husband's on his wedding night. I sink against the pillows, glad for the dim quiet of this room. There doesn't need to be any other stimulation for my senses than what this man will give me. Reverently, he traces the lines of my body with his hands, and I see no gray in his hair. His face is unlined. What did I think I saw earlier? And there's no hint of awkwardness, of the stiff formality I noticed the night we met. Before me is a wild creature, an uninhibited man I want desperately. He is definitive.

Still we don't speak.

We wrestle in deliciously scented sheets, kissing, tasting every inch of each other. He straddles my chest, feeds his cock to me inch by inch, takes mine in his mouth. Our bodies dance together in a lecherous dream. I slurp him down, his seed fills my mouth. Groaning, I detonate into his. This bed is a cloud, and I sink into unconscious fog.

It's nighttime when I wake to candlelight. He kneels between my legs. I can't remember my own name. My limbs float with bliss, my cock begs for another release, my head is full of him. Inside me is unnamable ravenousness. I've been fucked before—my college boyfriend begged until I gave in. A couple guys since. This isn't the same.

If I don't have this man inside me, I'll cease to exist.

First he bends his face to my ass while stroking himself. I feel his warm tongue exploring, staking a claim like I've done so many times. The pleasure is unbearable. Every inch of my body itches, from my hole to the tips of my toes, wriggling in the darkness.

Now my ankles are on his shoulders, and he eases in one of his long fingers, then a second. I feel his strength as he finds that secret place inside. A spark ignites there, the heat consumes me until I'm hyperaware of every cell in my body. My consciousness soars.

I watch his corded neck, veined arms, his broad but sloping shoulders move as he spits into his hand, lubricating his prick. A faint, crooked smile plays on his face, his eyes are heavy lidded as he connects with the point of entry. I hear myself cry out with pain—he's the opposite of gentle—it doesn't matter.

I give myself—his for the taking.

A guttural moan escapes me as I push toward him. He thrusts, entering fully, brutally. He raises an eyebrow, but isn't asking whether he may continue. He sees he's hurting me, knows I want him to. I squirm against the plains of his hard thighs.

Hiddleston remains silent, taking my ankles in his vise-like grip. He pulls back, strikes again, drives himself to my core. He slicks his hand and seizes my cock.

Mercilessly, he strokes; I shudder under his touch. He snakes his hips, impaling me with grievous force. His face contracts, a furious roar bursts from his chest. Seeing this, I shoot off into the air, jets of hot jizz hit my chest, spot the headboard and sheets, spill over Hiddleston's fingers. He cleans them with his predatory tongue.

He has lost control. His fearsome strength overwhelms and he pours himself into me, displacing the power of my body. Without warning, I'm in two places—flat on my back, dominated by this enthralling man—and somehow in the air around us. I feel him thrust into me once more, smell the lush sweat of his skin. Riveted by his animal gaze, I see myself, too.

I know this is uncommon. I spot the mole that shows in the mirror when I lift my chin to shave my neck. I see the downy hair at the small of Hiddleston's back, mark the flexing muscles of his rounded pale ass when he shoves his cock in to the hilt. And I watch myself fading like flower, pressed between the pages.

Still deep inside me, he latches his mouth onto mine. I live for eternity in that agonizing kiss. He drains the breath from my body. A rending noise buzzes in my head as I watch my chest collapse. It takes only moments for my limbs to waste away. I try to cry out, but it's far too late.

When he has regained his senses, Hiddleston carefully wraps me in a sheet. With a wave of his hand, a tall door opens in the bedroom's paneled walls. Behind it is a narrow staircase, impeccably free of dust like the rest of his townhouse. He ascends to the attic, a shrouded husk in his arms.

Seven plain wooden boxes rest there on the floor. The lids of six are sensibly shut. Placing me in the seventh, Hiddleston wears a look of fulfilled contrition. Hovering, diminishing, I observe him. Handsome, beardless and smooth, his is the regretful face of a young demigod.

"Sorry, Zach," he murmurs to me. "I meant to keep you longer, but couldn't help myself. You were irresistible."

LITTLE SUCKER

Rob Rosen

I was just passing through Transylvania, heading down Highway 65. Oh, and, no, not *that* Transylvania, by the way. Nope, this one was barely a blip on the map in the northeast corner of Louisiana, just a stone's throw away from the mighty Mississippi. Still, it was worth stopping at, if only for the kitsch factor, which the town, if you could call it that, played up to the hilt.

"Velcome, velcome," said the general store proprietor, in what could only be called a hick Romanian accent, his face an ashen white, dried blood (ketchup?) on his chin. "I vant to suck your blood."

I grinned. "My wallet, more likely."

He shrugged and promptly dropped the act. "Dracula T-shirts on sale: two for five and a quarter."

"Why would I need two?" I asked.

The shrug remained. "Heck, why would you need one?"

I gave him six crisp dollar bills and told him to keep the change. He only had the T-shirts in smalls and extra larges. Thankfully, my nephews ranged on the former side. "What's with the name?" I asked. "Transylvania, I mean? Some sort of marketing gimmick?"

He rang up my order and dropped the shirts into a plastic bag. "Named after the university in Lexington, Kentucky. You ever heard of it?"

I shook my head. "Nope."

"Welcome to the club," he said with a heavy sigh. "Still …"

I leaned in. "Still what?"

He held out a pair of glow in the dark vampire fangs. "Two for a dollar."

I plopped down my buck. "Still what?"

His huckster smile all but vanished as he also leaned in. "Well, the way I hear it told, there were, in fact, vampires here back in the day. Most of 'em got themselves hung just after the town got its neat little name."

"So, it's *not* named after the university?"

His shrug turned nod. "Nope, that part is true. But the way folks figured it, the vampires came when they heard about the town name. Maybe they thought there was some sort of association. Makes sense, right?"

I forced a grin. "Um, yeah. Makes sense." Then I paused, something suddenly nagging at me. "Wait, you said *most of 'em*. Some got away?" OK, so I'm a tad gullible. So sue me.

His nodding continued. "Just one. For some reason, the noose didn't work. Sucker—pardon the expression—got away."

In for a penny, in for a pound, I figured, so I asked, "To where?"

The nodding abruptly halted. "Eagle Lake, they all thought. Across the Mississippi, not too far from here. River was swollen at the time he escaped. By the time it ebbed, the town had forgotten all about him. Out of sight …"

I gulped. "Out of mind." But not out of mine, seeing as Eagle Lake was exactly where I was headed to, a distant cousin's cabin made available for a week's retreat. A cold shiver suddenly raced down my spine. "Got any wooden stakes, by the way?"

90

He plopped them down on the counter. "Two for ten."

"Why would I need two? Wouldn't one do the trick? That is, if I happened to encounter a vampire?"

Again he shrugged. "What if you were to miss?"

I handed him the ten. "Good …" I touched the tip of the nearest stake. "Point."

He grinned. "Funny."

Sadly, I wasn't trying to be.

An hour plus some change later I made it to the aptly named lake. An American bald eagle was circling my cabin as I pulled up. I smiled as I stared up at it and again when I stared down at the stakes still sitting in the passenger seat.

"Well, maybe you'll be helpful if I decide to pitch a tent." I gazed down at my crotch, which had strangely swelled and pulsed at the comment. "OK, now *that* was funny."

And, seeing as it was just me and the cabin and that soaring eagle out there, my pants slid off and my cock sprung out, the head already leaking, my balls hot and heavy from all the heat and humidity. Which meant that my T-shirt got hiked up and off next, leaving me in nothing but sneakers and socks and a boner that could fell a tree—though what a waste of a perfectly good boner that would've been. Ditto for the tree.

In any case, out of the car I went, my belongings still in the trunk, turgid cock leading me inside the cabin—which, by the way, had seen better days. Let's say the seventies—and 1870s at that. See, I'd let it be known that I needed a private, quiet space to catch up on some work, and my cousin heard the call and offered up this place, saying no one had used it in ages. Poking my head inside the cabin, ages seemed like a gross understatement. Emphasis on the gross.

"Hello?" I whispered as I entered. "Anybody home?" Or alive? Or wanting to hack me to death?

Thankfully, I got no reply, save for my cock bouncing and throbbing, aimed dead, as it were, ahead. I gave it a stroke and a thwack, sending it reeling. When it came to a standstill, it was again aimed at the rear wall of the cabin.

I sidestepped ancient, threadbare furniture, my sneakers leaving tracks in the layers of dust. I coughed as I kicked a cloud of it up into the air. "Maid have the century off?" I hacked.

Making my way across the cabin floor, I stared down at my dick, which was still aiming at the wall, still rigid and coursing with blood. I grabbed it, a million volts of adrenaline rushing through me, eyelids fluttering in response. "Sorry, fella," I told it. "End of the line." I knocked on the wall to offer up proof and was greeted by a rather unusual sound in return, almost like an echo, coming from the opposite side. "Hollow? Now that's weird." I stared down at my near nakedness, at my cock thick in my grip. "Well, *weirder*, at any rate."

I knocked yet again, harder this time, a noticeable dent left in my fist's wake. Given the age of the place, not to mention the state it was in, this wasn't at all surprising. Which meant that when I kicked it and a good part of the wall came crashing down, that, too, wasn't at all surprising. Of course, the man resting atop the granite counter on the other side of said wall, well, yes, *that* was surprising. And, again, we'll go with gross understatement on that one, also again with an emphasis on the gross part, mainly because he looked quite dead. As a doornail, in fact.

"Mister?" I whispered, swallowing hard as my hands swiped the air, clearing my way through the cloud of dust. "Are you, um ... well, do you need, um ..." I drew nearer, nearer still, until I was standing over him, the light from inside the cabin illuminating his otherwise alabaster face, the rest of his body covered in a black suit and equally black cape.

Gingerly, I placed my fingers on his exposed wrist, just like they do in the movies. The guy was ice cold but strangely pliable. Meaning, neither rigor nor mortis had paid a visit. Which was odd because he'd clearly been behind the wall for quite some time. Then again, considering he wasn't a mummy or a pile of ash (as in ashes to ashes), odd seemed fairly par for the course thus far. Odd, in fact, was a hole in one.

Again I stared down the length of him, which, all things considered, didn't take all that long. The guy couldn't have been more than five feet tall, even with the spiffy black shoes and the nifty black, jacked-up hairdo. Still, he was oddly—yes, there goes that word again—attractive, with a square jaw and cheekbones to die—no pun intended—for, and not a single freckle or mole or crease on his otherwise lifeless face. Heck, even my dick seemed to like him, seeing as it was still hovering at a ninety degree angle, give or take a degree or two, like a divining rod in search of ashen flesh instead of water.

Still, there was one place I hadn't searched just yet, one place that would've been the ultimate clue as to who, what, where, and why this guy was. And so, hands trembling, dick as well, I placed my fingers at the corner of his mouth and slowly lifted his upper lip.

"Holy cow," I managed, my voice barely above a whisper. "Or maybe make that bat." Because this guy had one hell of a pair of canines, long and sharp and …"lethal." I gulped at the word, then slowly, quietly, backed out of the, dare I say, *crypt* and hightailed it to my car, the wooden stakes quickly retrieved, just in case.

Now all I had to do was walk back in and plunge at least one of the stakes through his heart. Easy peasy, right? I mean, how difficult could it be do sink a slab of wood into someone? Not like he'd be resisting. Not like he'd even know. In fact, only I would know, more than likely. Know, that is to say, that I slaughtered someone while he lay helpless. Sleeping, really.

"Fuck," I cursed as I again stood over him. "Who am I kidding? I can't even kill a spider, let alone an entire human bat." I set the stakes down and ran my hand across his smooth forehead, a chill rushing through me that made my cock bounce. "Maybe you're not even evil or anything. Maybe you've never killed anyone. Maybe you just suck a little."

I stared at my hand and then at the top button of his starched white shirt. "A little peak couldn't hurt, though, would it?" My hand slid from his face to his chest. "I mean, technically, you're not even dead, so a little look-see wouldn't be, uh, creepy, right?" I nodded and popped open the top button. "Right." And when one button pops, another one is usually quick to follow, until, well, a look-see becomes an entire *Look! See!*

My little vampire was spot-on perfect, at least from nipple to nipple and chin to belly button. Not even Michelangelo could've carved anything so flawless, so unblemished, so, OK, *hot.* And, considering how arctic cold he was, hot was really saying something.

"But does the basement match the attic?"

OK, so fine, the little head was now in control of the big head, but in for a penny, in for a pound I always say. Or at least I just started saying, but still. In other words, I dropped his cape to the dusty floor, unbuckled his belt, unbuttoned the top button of his slacks, and *zzzipped* down his fly, the sound causing my cock to pulse, to drip copious amounts of pre-cum, which might've been aided by my now rapidly stroking fist.

His shoes came off next. Size six. I looked. Socks next, revealing white feet as smooth as silk, not even an errant hangnail, his tiny toes so cute that it was almost impossible not to suck on them. And, yes, fine, I sucked on them, so sue me.

Then I grabbed the hems of his slacks and yanked and pulled and tugged, inching them down his etched thighs and hairless legs and muscle-dense calves, until they were off and he was in nothing but white boxers and a completely parted white shirt: an Adonis in miniature, to be sure.

My hands were shaking as I grabbed the waistband of his pristine white boxers. With a slight tug, a trimmed ebony bush was revealed, the base of his shaft after that, and then, with a mighty yank, save for his shirt, he was lock, stock, and barrel naked. That is to say, he was locked in time and space, was utterly stock still, and had a dick that resembled a barrel: short and thick and round, with balls the size of ripened plums that now hung to the granite slab below.

He was, as previously noted, perfection.

"So, what do I do with you now, little vampire dude?" I asked, my voice the only sound in the dusty, small, dilapidated chamber. I sighed as I gazed upon him, at his finely chiseled body, held, I knew, somewhere between life and death, and then I sunk to the floor, legs out, my back to the granite base. "What do I do with you now?" It beared repeating.

It also didn't need to be asked a third and final time.

See, when I sunk, my foot stretching out, the tiniest of splinters jammed into my heel. I held my foot up and spotted the intruder, a barely discernible droplet of blood seeping out of the wound a second later.

I froze upon hearing the rustling, my muscles locked in fear, heart beating out a mad samba in my rapidly expanding and contracting chest. I turned my neck to the side and looked up, the shirt shaking as it hung down, the tiny toes squiggling.

"Hello?" I heard, the voice so faint that it could've easily been the wind playing tricks one me. If there was any wind, I mean. Which, suffice it say, there wasn't any, what with crypts being generally breezeless and all. "I ... *smell* ... you."

Slowly I stood, legs buckling, knees quaking, hard-on miraculously still in one steely piece. This time when I gazed down upon him, he was gazing back up at me with eyes so blue that they put the sky to shame, his teeth a gleaming white as he smiled my way, those fangs of his glinting in the meager light.

"Um, hi," I managed to squeak out.

His grin widened, hand falling off the slab before coming to a rest on my throbbing prick. I jumped but otherwise stayed put, even when his fingers wrapped around my turgid flesh and gave a weak tug. "I hear it, you know," he whispered, voice frail.

"Hear it?" I tilted my ear up to the ceiling. "Hear what?"

"The blood." He gave my cock a squeeze. "In here. Smell it, too. Can almost taste it."

I cringed at the imagery. "Um, yeah, you're so *not* going to drink blood from my dick, little vampire dude."

His grin remained, as did his hand on my cock. "I just need a drop, the tiniest pinprick of it." He paused and then, it seemed, read my mind. "And then you may fuck me."

I reached out my hand and fondled his willy, then his balls, and lastly the satiny smooth crack that ran beneath it all. "Or I could just fuck you now and call it a day. I mean, you're up and all." I flicked his dick from side to side. "Well, not so much up as awake."

He nodded, feebly. "Though *up* is so much more fun, yes?" That last word slithered inside my mind, seeking a toehold, something to grab on to.

"Yes," I replied, fairly mesmerized, not to mention leaking up a storm. Then I shook my head, trying as best I could to regain my senses. "I mean, uh, no. Then you'll suck me dry, and not in a good way."

He chuckled, wheezed, coughed. He was conscious, but barely back within the land of the living. And so I bent down and retrieved one of the wooden stakes. Then I put his hand back on my cock. Because, though dazed and confused, I was also horny as all hell. I set the tip of the stake just over his heart and pushed slightly down.

He winced. Then I winced. "You can't, won't," he rasped.

"Though I have to," I replied. "It's for the greater good. Namely my greater good health."

His chuckled repeated, as did the grip on my dick. "Kiss me first."

It sounded like a trick. It sounded like certain death. Oh, and it also sounded like a slice of heaven—a la mode, with a cherry on top. In other words, with his hand still wrapped around my impossibly hard cock, I bent down and touched my lips to his, which was about as close to landing on a cloud as a guy could get.

In fact, it was impossible to break from such a kiss, which was, not surprisingly, about as perfect as he was, and, sadly, just as short. Because as soon as our lips meshed, his tongue thrashing inside my mouth, skyrockets taking flight behind my fluttering eyelids, I suddenly felt his canines sinking into my lower lip, tasted the blood as it spurted inside my mouth, not to mention inside his mouth.

He broke the kiss first. I stared down at him, still very much enraptured. "Uh-oh," I hummed, swiping my tongue across my bloody lip. "That can't be good."

His eyes burned like bonfires now. "Really? Look down."

I stood there, my eyes moving from his impossibly handsome face, down his pearl-white chest and belly, until they finally landed on his mast of a prick, which was now no longer flaccid but hard and thick and very much vertical. "Guess you're more of a grower than a shower."

He grinned. "You may suck it, if you like."

"A final meal?" I hazarded to ask as I hopped on the slab and positioned myself between his hairless, stunted legs. "You can't kill me—I brought you back."

But still he replied with the enigmatic, "We shall see."

I sighed. If it was a final meal, at least it was an appetizing one. In other words, down my mouth went, engulfing him whole, his splendid cock filling every centimeter before a gagging tear meandered its way down my cheek. I popped his prick out of my mouth. It shown, spit-slick, like a flame, yours truly being the moth.

I hiked his legs up, his diminutive feet now planted on my back. I stared hungrily at his cock and balls and pink, puckered, perfect hole. So many choices. So little time? Well now, that was indeed the question, though it remained in the back of my head as the front of my head eagerly went down on his tender chute.

While I jacked his prick, I rimmed him out with gusto, licking and slurping and nibbling on his ring. By then, I longed to taste it, to enter it with tongue and finger and cock and anything else I could shove up there, to at last be one with him.

And so, in my tongue slid, a moan escaping from between his lips that made my head spin. A finger slid inside next, his chute gripping my digit, then the next one, and the one after that, until I was triple-digit pumping his hole with one hand and his impossibly thick cock with the other, my eyes fairly glued, stapled, and cemented to the scene unfolding before me.

"Fuck me," he soon commanded.

"You read my mind," I cooed.

He laughed. "Yes, I know."

His legs came off my shoulders, feet now wide to the side, hole winking my way, still slick with spit. My cock slipped inside of him, no preamble, no gentle teasing of my throbbing, mushroomed head, just one steady glide and I was in like Flynn. Down his ass sunk, up his back went, until we were chest to chest, the little jockey riding his prized pony with wild abandon, while I in turn bucked and fucked and rocketed my cock deep, deep, *deep* inside of him.

His eyes were now locked with mine, tethering me to him. "A very nice way to wake from a long slumber," he purred, jacking my cock with his exceedingly talented hole.

"About that," I grunted. "How exactly did you escape the hangman's noose to arrive here, in said slumber?"

He laughed. "Small neck, I suppose. I simply slid out, killed a dozen or so of them, and then found this cabin."

My cock plowed into him. He writhed and moaned so loudly that the walls shook. "And here you've slept this entire time?"

He nodded, sighed, pumping his prick now. "It wasn't safe to venture back into town. And without sustenance, I fell into silent sleep. Until …"

It was my turn to nod. "Until I found you." The kiss was like no other, as if it reached into my very soul and twisted it into submission. "Seems a shame to lose me then, so soon after we just got, um, acquainted."

He sighed, his hand temporarily motionless on his prick, ass no longer pounding into my crotch. "But the blood, it wasn't enough, not nearly. I need more, and then more after that, and more after that."

I smiled, the kiss repeated, again and again and again. "And without getting caught by the locals this time around."

"Exactly." His fist went into overdrive on his prized prick, my cock now at his hilt, our bodies as one, until it was impossible to tell where I ended and he began. "Do they still hang vampires back in town?"

I shook my head. "No vampires left. Just you. Not much of a town either." And still I smiled, an idea forming in my much-addled brain. "But lots and lots of tourists, all willing to pay for a piece of vampire lore."

He didn't cum—not in gooey aromatic spurts, that is—but he did climax. His head tossed back, his eyelids shut tight, and his jaw went slack just before he howled. At that same instant, my own cock spewed. Suffice it to say, he sucked every last drop of sustaining semen into his tight little vampire ass. No, it wasn't blood, but it seemed to do in a pinch, the fire in his eyes suddenly blazing like the sun as my, shall we say, life-force moved from me and into him.

"Well now," he groaned into my ear, "that's something new."

I hugged him tight. "So you don't need to kill me after all?"

"Such a waste that would've been."

I sighed. "Tell me about it."

"I thought I just did," he quipped. "And what's a 'tourist' …?"

The cabin fixed up nicely, what with two of us fixing it up and all. Plus, Vlad, my little sucker's name—very old school, yes, but Vlad, to put it mildly, was very old—had enough vim and vigor, not to mention a daily dose of spunk up his stellar tush, to get it done in record timing.

After that, wouldn't you know it, but he also got a part time job at the convenience store back in Transylvania. Seems like it's awfully hard to say no to the little fellow. Go figure. See, he really did need blood, at least in big enough doses, and if he tried to get it from me, there was always the chance that he wouldn't be able to stop sucking. And if he didn't stop said sucking, well, it's pretty easy to imagine what would happen next: Corpse City. And no one wanted—or needed—that headache, me especially.

"Velcome, velcome," Vald would say when a tourist wandered into the store, in what could only be called an honest to goodness Romanian accent, his face an ashen white, dried blood (nope, not ketchup!) on his chin. "I vant to suck your blood."

And, really, what Vlad vants, Vlad gets. Present company included. Then he'd suck just what he needed and I'd jab him with one of those handy dandy wooden stakes to remind him to stop. The tourist would promptly forget what just happened and usually leave with two discounted small or extra large T-shirts, a couple of glow-in-the-dark vampire teeth, and, yes, two wooden stakes.

Not surprisingly, business was suddenly booming.

Also not surprisingly, I never went home again after that. As in, you guessed it, forever never. Because forever was what Vlad and I now seemed to have. Last and final time: go figure.

BLACK SNOW

Mark Wildyr

We'd been nuts to tackle fifty kilometers for our first cross-country run, but we had it made now. A hop off the bluff and two easy klicks downhill to the Blazer. Simon Manz and I—both juniors at the University of New Mexico—were rated Alpine skiers, but this was something poles apart … different equipment, different skills, and different muscles.

Sim leaned on his sticks, downing sausage for protein and fortified chocolate for quick energy. "Damn, O, this place gives me the creeps. Never seen a forest so quiet." "O" was his shorthand for my name, Owen Ohlren. He pointed at a black smudge lying across a berm of white snow. "What the hell is that?"

"A log?" I was too tired to indulge my curiosity.

"Uh-uh. That's no log."

My flesh puckered from head to toe as the abnormality faded away. "Let's go," I said, trying not to sound spooked.

I went over first and heard Sim plop onto the pillow of snow behind me. The exhilaration of schussing down a black diamond trail with my best friend exorcised the nameless fear of a moment before. Unaccustomed to the cross-country bindings and low-cut shoes, I concentrated on making my feet go where I wanted, trusting the skis to follow. Narrower blades and the lack of steel edges gave the boards a different bite, but they carved a sculpted track as I dodged trees and absorbed moguls.

My joy was given voice by a war hoop behind me. A minute later, I knifed a double S in the meadow where my Chevy Blazer sat beneath a half-inch of new snow. Giving a cry of triumph, I glanced back up the wooded slope. No Sim.

He was rated a solid nine, too good to have fallen or kissed a tree. But accidents happen to anyone, even tens. I labored up the lesser inclines by pushing myself with the poles. As the terrain became steeper, I duck-walked. Then changed to a side step.

I found his tracks shooting straight down the fall line. Then he'd gone into a sudden snowplow followed by a christie right through some brush. I pushed off in the wake of his erratic trail and found him sprawled stark naked on his belly in a mound of snow. Near his side, a patch of black snow faded away. Scared out of my wits, I knelt beside him and grabbed his clothing. As soon as I put a hand on his back, he screamed.

"It's me, Sim! It's O!"

"Why'd you do that to me? Why?"

"Do what?" I brushed ice crystals off him. He settled down and let me dress him.

Hypothermia could kill. Once the body's core temperature started dropping from dampness and exposure and exhaustion, it continued to fall until you did something to stop it. When it hit eighty-one, you were dead. The symptoms were already there: confusion, lack of muscle control, fuzzy thinking.

Cursing his three-pin bindings, I finally managed to get his skis reattached, pulled him to his feet, and hugged him tight against my side. We came off the slope that way.

Once he was safely in the Blazer, I flipped the headlights on and glimpsed an indistinct figure at the extreme edge of their reach. I threw the vehicle in four-wheel and crept forward. As the lights advanced, they picked up a bar of that eerie, disappearing black snow.

I fed the engine gas, bouncing recklessly across the meadow onto the icy road. Sim was worse, delirious. Then he mumbled something that almost cost me control of the wheel.

"Why'd you rape me, man?"

"What? Hey, I didn't rape anybody!"

He needed a doctor, but how could I take him to one while he was accusing me of rape?

I registered at the first motel I saw in the little town of Cuba and hustled him inside a room. I stripped him and immersed him in a tub of hot water. While the wet heat did its thing, I piled every blanket I could find on the bed and put the last of our warming chemicals between the sheets.

I stripped naked to haul him out of the tub rather than get my clothing wet. He stood docilely while I rubbed his buffed, sleek form dry. He curled into the fetal position when I tucked him in bed. The shivering had started again, so I spooned myself to his back until the tremors stopped. After a few minutes, I grew aware I held a naked, hunky Simon Manz in my arms. Hard cock against his ass, my piss slit tingled from the contact. My glans warmed to his touch. What would it be like to do something more than cuddle?

His buttocks shifted against my erection. He moaned my name. I pulled him closer and murmured reassurances. His hand fumbled at my groin. His grip on my hard shaft sent shivers through my body. Damn, he was positioning my cock. My tip penetrated the folds of his crack, overcoming the warm, wet resistance as he shoved his butt against me. My dick slid into his bowels. It wasn't enough! I thrust against him, entering him more deeply.

After two years of unacknowledged lust, I was fucking my best friend. I withdrew and savored the entry again. Then I lunged against him as his butt met my thrusts. I grasped his big, hot cock and held him loosely, masturbating him with every lunge of my body.

I eased him onto his belly. Pushing his legs apart with my knees, I entered him for the third delicious time, deeper than before. The magic began in my arches, crept up my calves, seized my thighs, and took possession of my balls. Electric currents short-circuited my system. Muscles contracted. Cum exploded out of my cock, and I swear there was a recoil like a shotgun blast. Sim grunted once and convulsed in the throes of his own orgasm, rendering me a helpless mass of jelly. It was quiet in the room except for labored breathing. And then, "Why'd you leave me to freeze to death, O?"

Simon wouldn't have anything to do with me after that. My best friend had cut me off. All he'd said on the drive back to Albuquerque was he'd come straight down the fall line when I stepped out of the bushes. After he wrecked, I'd torn off his clothing and violently rammed my cock up his ass.

He refused to acknowledge what happened in the motel room. *That* sure as hell hadn't been rape. By the time we reached UNM and unloaded our gear, I hoped a night's sleep would make things OK. But the next time I called, he hung up on me.

I needed answers to what had happened up on the mountain, so I loaded the Blazer on Saturday and took off alone. Parking in the exact spot where we had before, I examined our fuzzy tracks. After strapping on skis, I set out in a steady step-push-glide over the trail we'd broken the previous week until I reached the jump-off where we turned south on our downhill run. The place emitted an eerie atmosphere. The air wasn't quite right. The forest seemed to watch me malevolently. The hair on my neck rose. A movement to my right startled me. I whirled. Nothing there. Except a strip of ebony.

Heart pounding, blood racing, I pushed over the edge. Going into a bent-knee crouch, I shot straight down the fall line, leaning left and right to avoid trees. Just above the point where Sim had crashed, someone stepped out of the bushes and blocked my way. Simon Manz stared straight up the hill as I came hurtling toward him.

Expecting something like this, I shot by him on the left and opened up to the max. When I hit the meadow, I went into a snowplow and halted beside my car.

Sim's Toyota was nowhere in sight. I glanced back up the slope. No sign of him. Still, I was frantic to be out of there. As I clawed the car door open, something appeared in the gathering dusk at the corner of my eye. Grabbing a mag light from the front seat, I swung around. Sim stood not five feet away. The bright light hit him squarely in the face. He cried out and clawed his eyes as he lurched away from the beam.

An adrenalin rush practically propelled me into the Blazer. Spooked out of my mind, I ground the starter, threw the truck in gear, and abandoned Sim to his fate.

A dark figure appeared ahead of me. Sim! His handsome features twisted as he threw up his hands. I hit the brake, but the vehicle skated forward. There was no sound, no cry, no thump, no nothing as the Blazer slammed right over him. I regained control and steered in a wide circle, terrified of finding my friend's crumpled body. There was nothing. Nothing but black snow.

Losing all reason, I stomped on the accelerator and rocketed down the crooked mountain road, tires planing on skims of icy water. I shook like an aspen in a blizzard all the way to Cuba.

In need of something hot, I parked in front of a café and scooted through the door to claim a seat at the counter. When my shakes subsided, I fumbled for my cell phone. A sleepy voice answered my call. I glanced at the clock on the wall. Nearly midnight? Where had the time gone?

"Simon, is that you?"

"Who the hell else would it be?"

"God! I'm glad to hear your voice!" I drew a shaky breath and told him what had happened.

"Don't talk crap, Ohlren. Make sense."

"I will. Meet me at eleven in my room tomorrow, OK?" I snapped the phone shut before he could refuse. A mug of coffee braced me some, but there was still a chill down my back. The chunky Hispanic waitress with tired, baggy eyes regarded me curiously as she poured me seconds.

"Seen your rig outside. Been skiing up on Cerro Sangriento?" She frowned when I nodded. "Not such a good place, Bloody Peak."

"Is that what it means? Bloody Peak?"

"Something happen up there?"

I tried to laugh. "Just got spooked, I guess. Black snow. That *disappears*."

"I seen it once. And just 'fore I did, I thought I seen somebody. Then he wasn't there no more. Just that black soot on the snow." She stirred like she was coming out of a reverie. "I don't go above the Plata no more."

"The river? Why?"

She rubbed a purple-blushed eyelid. "Know what Rio La Plata means?"

"Silver River."

"That 'cause silver leaches into the water. Ain't enough to mine, but maybe enough to keep evil penned up on that rock."

"Can you put a name to the evil?"

"What's afraid of silver?"

Feeling ludicrous, I answered. "Werewolves? You know, a silver bullet."

"Ain't just wolf-people scared of silver bullets."

"Vampires?" I ventured.

"You said it, not me. But there ain't no sheep or cattle north of the Plata. That oughta tell ya something." She cast an eye on me. "I got something for you in case you go up again." She disappeared into the kitchen and returned with a small burlap bag. "Might come in handy."

I got on the road soon after, battling sleep and exhaustion on the two-hour drive to campus. I staggered into my dorm, took a shower, and flopped into bed. The next thing I knew, Sim was banging on my door.

He claimed the chair and demanded to know what was going on. I settled cross-legged on the bed in my shorts and led him through my trip. "So, I didn't rape you, man. No more'n you stood in the middle of the trail and tried to make me wreck. No more'n I ran over you in the Blazer."

"Then who?"

"I don't know yet. But we're going back."

"You're crazy! You might not have got your ass raped, but I sure did."

"If you're so upset about what happened on the mountain, why did we do what we did in that motel room?"

Sim studied a fingernail. "He tore off my clothes and left me to die in the snow." He shifted his gaze to me. "I try not to think about that motel room, but can't keep from it. I was freezing until you hugged me— Fuck it! I wanted to feel you in me again!"

"Sim, I've wanted you since the day we met, but I didn't do it up on that mountain. And it wouldn't have happened in the motel if you hadn't reached back and touched me. Man, I couldn't believe I was inside you."

He looked into my eyes. "Me, neither. But it was great. Are we gonna do it again?"

I slid off the bed and pulled him to his feet. Our first kiss shocked both of us, but it was a pleasant, reach-down-in-your-guts shock. Sim's naked flesh excited me something fierce. He was fucking beautiful. My cock was like a steel rod when he slipped my jockeys down.

My penis was straight, his curved upward. We pressed our hips together. I clutched him to me, holding him by the buns. His hands clasped my waist. I tipped us over onto the bed.

He moved to my nipples and showed me what girls all over the globe already knew … it got to you. Then his lips closed over my glans. When he wrapped his tongue around my shaft, I rolled my hips. Watching my cock slide in and out of his mouth was a rush.

I ran my hands down his broad back and inhaled the scent of his shampoo. All my senses were engaged, stimulated, overloaded. Gasping a warning, I spasmed. Cum shot through me in rivulets, choking him. Groaning, I fucked his mouth until my convulsions passed. Then I fell back on the bed and gasped for air.

Sim scissored his legs on the outside of mine and humped my groin, burying his handsome face in my neck. I stroked his straining torso, tolerant of his desperate need. By the time he grunted and held himself hard against me, I was raging again. I waited until he flooded my belly before dipping my dick in his slick cum, raising his legs, and putting it to his sphincter.

I fucked for half an hour, both of us slick from perspiration and cum, until he got a raging hard-on and beat his own meat. I fucked until he shot again, and then I lost it, lubing his black hole with another heavy load.

"Gonna start calling you Double O because you sure as shit shoot buckshot!" He pressed his head against my cheek. "You realize we'd probably never got together without that thing up on the mountain?"

We left Albuquerque at four the following Saturday morning.

"Sim, if that thing up there's a vampire, how'd we get away from him?"

He considered the question a moment. "Wasn't quite dark. Maybe that made a difference. I don't think he functions in daylight."

He picked up the bag the waitress had given me and let out a squeal, about sending the Blazer off the road. "Look at all this crap! Crucifix. Bible. Garlands of garlic. Nails painted silver. Bag of salt. A couple of railroad flares. Oh, yeah. And a wooden stake."

When we crossed the La Plata, I started hunting for private land. It made more sense the creature's den was on private, not public land. We used up most of the day locating a tract near the peak with a building hidden in a thick copse of conifers surrounded by a fence.

"What now?" Sim asked. "Go up and knock on the door?"

"Sounds like a plan."

Armed with a heavy flashlight and bag of odds and ends, we climbed the padlocked gate and went vampire hunting. The woods were eerily quiet. The snow had degraded badly in the clearing before the cabin—what skiers calls crud. There weren't more than a couple of hours of sunlight left.

The building was a sturdy, two-story log affair larger than most mountain cabins. An old-fashioned bell with a pull rope dangled beside the door frame. When I tugged on the cord, the bell gave a tinny clank.

When no one appeared at the door, I tried the latch. It was un-locked. With Sim hard on my heels, I stepped through the portal into near-total darkness. My powerful mag merely sliced a thin swath through the black interior. I was reminded of a nave in a colonial mis-sion church. Occasional shafts of pale light outlined a few blackened clerestory windows, but otherwise it was midnight in there—even though there was sunlight outside.

I stepped through a room that must have been forty feet long. The door at the far end was likely the kitchen or eating area. The atmosphere was so heavy it absorbed light rays.

A noise hauled me up short. The hair on my neck rose. My butt puckered. I turned to flee but steadied myself. The kitchen door squeaked loudly when I pushed it open. The room was empty. I called Sim, who stumbled forward.

"Isn't there a light in this place?" His raspy whisper cut through the darkness.

"Keep your eye on the front door," I said. "I'm going to the room on our right."

Despite my brave words, I didn't want to open that door. Somehow I understood this was its nest. I was a mass of gooseflesh. My puckers had puckers. The hair on my arms and neck rose. I slipped through the door and came to an abrupt halt.

The flashlight revealed a spacious bedroom as I swung the light in a slow arc. No wooden coffin for this vampire. A huge four-poster bed covered by a heavy, ornate canopy dominated the room. This room had a different feel. Someone lived here.

The uncanny darkness, the preternatural stillness, turned my blood cold. My ass itched unbearably. My stomach fell right down to the floor. *There was someone here.* Recoiling at movement on the periphery of my vision, I caught a glimpse of Sim.

"Man," I whispered. "You scared the shit out of me! Looks like this is the old boy's bedroom. Would you look at that bed?" Sim's palm on my back propelled me forward for a closer look. I put a hand to the silken cover. "It's still warm. He was here …" Suddenly, he shoved me roughly down on the bed. "That's not funny! Stop playing around." And then I was fighting for air as a strong hand held my head to the musty bed covers, my protests muffled by dusty silk.

His legs between mine, he rendered me helpless with only that incredible grip on my head. My belt bruised my flesh as my trousers were jerked down around my knees. Naked flesh probed my butt. A cock! A big, hard cock!

Shit! It wasn't Sim. It was that *thing!*

I shouted into the bedcovers as a red hot bar of steel penetrated me. My body arched against the pain, but he restrained me easily. When I stopped struggling, he relaxed his hold enough for me to draw gulps of dust-laden oxygen through the silk.

Hard thighs struck my ass as that rod savaged my insides. I fought to breathe, even as my mind reeled on the edge of unconsciousness.

Suddenly, there was an angry roar! The pressure eased. The thing invading my intestines was ripped out. I turned my head and pulled in air as sweet as a fresh, clean breeze on a downhill run. When I could think halfway clearly, I rolled onto my back.

Two Simons wrestled in the darkness. Snatching my trousers into place, I groped frantically for the flashlight and turned the mag into the eyes of the figure facing me.

"Shit, O!" Sim shouted, closing his eyes against the sudden glare.

I flashed on the other figure. The handsome features twisted into a hard, cruel, foreign face. A bloody stake protruded from the creature's powerful, naked back. Despite the wound and trying to avoid the necklace of garlic cloves around Sim's neck, the creature was managing to overcome my friend.

Struggling to my feet, I brought the palm of my hand down to strike the blunt end of the wooden peg sticking out of the vampire's back. But the creature moved, and I merely slapped him hard on the spine. He howled and backhanded Sim into a corner before turning on me. I scrambled backward across the bed. The vampire stood for a moment, indistinct in the darkness except for the bright red pinprick of his eyes. Belatedly, I flashed the torch's beam in his face. He cried in pain and threw out his arm to shield his eyes even as he moved for me.

I slung the heavy flashlight as hard as I could. It shattered against his forehead, plunging the room into inky darkness. Ignoring his roar, I tumbled blindly across the bed and slammed my feet squarely into his chest. He reeled backward. I came up beside him, planting an elbow in his side as hard as I could. Once past the thing, I groped my way toward where I'd last seen Sim, praying he wasn't dead. Feeble scratching from the corner gave me hope. A powerful hand clasped my shoulder. Oh, God! *He had me.*

Suddenly, a pulsing red light flooded the room. The creature clawed at his eyes. Sim had lit one of the railroad flares. The vampire, in the guise of a handsome, muscled, naked man, swayed in the middle of the room, groaning in agony from the harsh light.

Spying the burlap bag at my feet, I rummaged around and seized the bag of salt. I tore it open and threw the contents in the vampire's face. An unearthly scream pierced the room. I thought for a moment he would rip out his eyeballs, but even in his pain, he blundered blindly toward me, so I drove a silver-painted nail into his thigh. He squalled like a child, but his rage drove him on. He caught me on the jaw, tumbling me like a blow-up toy.

Sim hauled me to my feet. Still dizzy, I wasn't aware of what he pressed into my hand until he shouted for me to light the second railroad flare.

Gathering strength from some ungodly source, the vampire slowly advanced, shading his eyes with one hand. His long, flaccid cock swung like a pendulum as he limped across the room. I waited until he had almost reached Sim before striking the flare.

Nothing happened! I tried it again. It took. The room danced anew from the sudden, overpowering flame. The creature shrank away from the searing fire. I lunged forward and jammed the flare deep into an eye socket. His agonized screech unnerved me.

The beast fell back on his bed, squirming and squealing. Sim tossed his own dying flare on a pillow near the vampire's head. The ancient silk caught and blossomed. Yellow tendrils of fire raced up the canopy. The vampire's body stiffened, the curve of the chest, the thick pubic hair, the erect cock were horrifyingly sensual. A spark fell, and the pubes caught fire. The beast screamed and suddenly disappeared! The unspent flare jammed into his eye and the bloody stake from his back dropped onto the empty bed. The vampire was gone … leaving a long black shadow to be consumed by flames.

Sim and I broke at the same time and raced for the front door. The sun had disappeared, but enough ambient light remained to guide us. We broke a three-minute mile getting back to the car. Neither of us looked back until we were in the Blazer, doors locked. I'm not sure what protection that afforded except the psychological kind.

Smoke poured from the house. After watching for a moment, we sped away and let it burn. Maybe whatever was in there would burn up, too.

Once we reached Cuba, I pulled into a motel. Neither of us had said much since fleeing the horror up on Cerro Sangriento. We showered separately, munched on some sausage sticks we habitually carried, and flopped on the bed.

"Shit!" Sim finally broke the silence.

"That pretty well covers it," I agreed. "Hell, we got a room and a bed. Might as well make use of them."

Simon Manz might not have screwed around with guys, but he knew a lot about fucking. We rolled around on the bed in that darkened motel room like two vampires in love, falling into an exhausted sleep only when sun backlit the thick drapes of our room.

THE COMING STORM

Vincent Lambert

"Damned sunshine!"

Devon squinted through the slats of his dusty louvered shutters. "When does that cleaning lady come again?" He mentally reviewed his datebook for Maria's next visit, and it wasn't for another week. He sighed and drew back into the cool darkness of his kitchen. Adjusting his burgundy pajamas, Devon strolled to the book-lined den. It was already late afternoon, but he was just starting his day. He plunked down in his favorite chair, turned on the TV, and looked at the screen. Another tropical storm was barreling toward the tip of Florida, but that didn't faze him as he'd weathered a storm or two in his time.

Devon had never planned on living in Key West, but it had been nearly five years since he'd made the Sunshine State his home. Since then, he had managed to maintain his pale, tan-free complexion— but only by careful planning. Devon and sunshine did not mix well.

Pushing back his thick salt-and-pepper hair, he got up and went to the kitchen. Another window was draped by heavy fabric. It looked out on the street and was sometimes Devon's only glimpse of his neighbors. He still hadn't met any of them, but that was by careful planning, too.

As he adjusted the band of his pajamas, he debated whether to have another cup of coffee. He felt his dick rubbing on his thigh but decided to ignore it and hit the shower instead. He had a long night ahead. *Hmm, where should I target tonight?* he wondered as he unbuttoned his top.

Tommy quickly buttoned the collar of his white dress shirt and pulled his plaid tie through the loop. He hated making a knot, but he had to look presentable when going out canvassing with his brother. Late afternoon sunlight streamed into his yellow bedroom as he stood in front of the mirror. The walls reflected the light and seemed to illuminate his blond hair and make his bright blue eyes shimmer. He had even shaved, not that he needed it. Tommy was a senior in college, but he barely had any whiskers on his baby face. As he adjusted the tie for a second time, he thought back to the night before. He had snuck out after dinner and driven into town.

The local gay bar was only a few miles from his parents' house, but Tommy had never been inside. The previous evening, he had circled its parking lot. Sitting in his dad's pickup, he watched as neighborhood guys entered. But he couldn't bring himself to go in. The crowd was mixed, but mostly older guys in jeans or sweats. He felt a strong pull to these men and was rarely attracted to guys his own age. Not that it mattered. He had barely kissed a guy *or* a girl. It's not that his religious beliefs forbade it, but it was frowned upon unless one was married. And the idea of being with a man—well, he didn't want to think about the repercussions of that. So after cruising the parking lot for twenty minutes, he drove home defeated.

A knock on his door jolted him back to his tie, now perfectly knotted and even. "We gotta go, Thomas." His brother, Ted, also dressed in

116

a shirt and tie, was at the door. "I was thinking we should head over by Duval Street today. We didn't hit that last week."

Tommy smoothed his hair and took one last look. Time to spread the good word.

Devon was toweling his hair dry when he heard voices from outside. There was rarely any activity on his quiet side street—only the hum of a lawnmower every Monday or the garbage truck that passed twice a week with a noisy din. He went to the front window and looked out. Two young men wearing neckties were walking up the block. One was taller and had curly hair, but Devon's eyes zoomed in on the other. He was small and slight but had a glow about him. His blond hair shone in the now dimming light. Devon could make out the lines of his lean body—it was lithe, like a dancer's—and he watched as the duo went from door to door.

What are these two selling? Devon wondered as he zipped up his black sweat suit and headed to the dark living room. He paused at the hallway mirror to arrange his hair. *Not bad for an old guy.* Moving past the kitchen, he turned on the hall light just as the doorbell rang. This was a rare sound around the house, and Devon flinched with slight annoyance. *I can't possibly answer,* he thought as he looked at his watch. Part of him was curious as to what the young men wanted, but he decided he couldn't risk it. He listened as the bell chimed again, and he heard the boys talking. He stood behind the door.

Tommy's shirt was visibly soaked with sweat as he and Ted walked the balmy streets. They did this together twice a week: going to different neighborhoods to hand out pamphlets and talk to community members about their church. It was usually sunny and hot, but today a strong breeze shook the palm trees. *Maybe that storm is going to hit us,* Tommy thought as they went about their business. The humid air smacked him in the face, making him wish he could loosen his collar.

Ted coaxed his brother along. "C'mon, Tom, we gotta finish up before it gets dark," he said as they approached a quaint bungalow at the end of the block.

"Doesn't look like anyone's home," Tommy said as they walked up the path. Just then a light in the hallway switched on. Ted walked to the door and rang. No answer.

"Should we just leave a flyer?" Tommy asked. After a moment, he rang again. A long, narrow window framed the door, but it was covered with a curtain. Tommy thought he saw movement inside, but no one came to the door.

"OK, let's go," Ted said as he turned toward the street. "Put a flyer in the box. We should get home for supper anyway." Tommy moved to follow but glanced back to see a pale hand with long, slender fingers pulling back the curtain. The glint of a gold ring with a large red stone caught his eye. "Hey, I think …" he started to call after Ted, but just as quickly, the curtain fell back in place. His brother was already halfway down the driveway. *Must be some old person who lives there,* Tommy thought. Catching up to Ted, he asked what they were having for dinner.

Devon had hovered by the door. Knowing the young men were so close, he couldn't resist and had pulled back the curtain for a look. Yes, the blond was even more delectable up close. His eyes were shiny and his skin perfectly clear. He vaguely reminded Devon of someone, though he couldn't place who. A furtive glance was all Devon allowed himself. He waited until he saw the boys walk away then switched on the porch light and opened the door. In the gathering darkness, he could see they had put something in his mailbox. He looked up and down the street before deciding it was safe to venture outside. There he found a small booklet, appearing to be religious in nature.

He looked at the cover, which showed a mountain range with a breaking sunrise behind it. Below the image, large type read: God's Love Never Dies. Devon rolled it up and took it inside with him. He was getting hungry. Time to dine.

The parking lot was more crowded than usual. Several cars were parked by the entrance of The Palm, and a streetlamp lit the front. *There's nothing as depressing as a gay bar on a Monday night,* Devon thought. He sat in the solitude of his black BMW, looking out through the tinted glass. As Frank Sinatra sang "Only the Lonely," Devon had a clear view of the comings and goings. *Same shit, different night.* He had seen his fair share of gay bars. They no longer appealed to him, but he had work to do. And sometimes this was where he did it.

He recognized a few locals that he had seen while shopping in town. From the outside, it looked like the usual assortment of older queens, tourists, and a few frat boys from the local community college. The latter were always his favorite. It took only a couple of drinks to loosen them up. That's when Devon could get what he needed. He turned off the engine and gathered himself. "Guess I better get busy," he thought as he got out of the car.

Inside the bar, loud music and dim lighting greeted him. A cluster of guys was gathered around a pool table playing a game. In the corner, a couple drank and necked. Devon kept walking. He was a man on a mission. He had a need and at least one of these unsuspecting men was going to fulfill it.

At the bar, he spotted three college dudes chatting with the bartender. They were dressed in shorts and flip-flops, with baseball caps hiding what Devon assumed was unruly hair. The guys were drinking beer as they talked and laughed. *Easy prey,* Devon thought as he sidled up to the bar. "Scotch rocks, please," he said to the bartender in his most elegant voice.

The guys stopped talking long enough to take in the new arrival. They watched as Devon paid for his drink and took a sip. He noticed that their conversation had stopped.

"Didn't mean to interrupt, guys," Devon said good-naturedly.

"No problem, man," the tallest one said. "We're just hanging out. How about you?"

Devon surveyed the three friends. He knew what he wanted from them, and he knew how to get it. Men were always horny, so that was usually a good place to start.

"Oh, just thought I'd come into town and enjoy some ... male companionship," Devon flirted. As he spoke, he made eye contact with the youths for the first time. His blue eyes burned into theirs, making them take notice in a way they hadn't before. He held their gaze. That's when one of the frats said, "Cool. Would you like to join us for a bonfire at the beach?"

A low moon hung over the winding path as Devon, pulling his jacket tighter against the rising wind, followed his new acquaintances. The ocean could be heard in the distance.

"This is where we usually set up," one of his three pickups said. Although they had exchanged names, he couldn't remember a one. *Must be old age,* he thought with a chuckle. Their names didn't matter. He was about to receive what mattered. But before that, he figured he might as well have some fun with them. The tallest frat boy was nearest to him as they walked. Devon looked up and said, "Full moon always makes me horny. How about you?" The beefy teen nodded his agreement. "Fuck yeah, man." That extra round Devon had bought was definitely working in his favor.

When they reached a spot behind a dune, the guys got to work building a fire. Soon the flames were raging and the trio started passing a joint, which Devon politely declined. The boys began joking and wrestling with one another. Their sweaty roughhousing was getting

Devon turned on. "Sure is hot down here," Devon said as he looked deep into the eyes of the blond student, who immediately started taking off his shirt, shoes, and jeans. When the boy was down to his tighty-whities, Devon allowed his eyes to linger on his broad shoulders and the way his curly hair fell around his neck. The other boys stripped down too, and Devon watched as they started pulling on their baggy boxers.

"Why don't we play a game?" Devon suggested. "How about we see who can get hard first?"

The tall frat chimed in: "Too late!" He snickered as he allowed his stiffy to show from the inside of his shorts. His cock head looked angry in the orange light.

"I guess you win," Devon said with a smile. Then he turned to the others. "How about you guys?" Their hard-ons were already evident. All they had to do was take them out. With one look from Devon, they complied. Three frat jocks with rock-hard dicks would be a wealth of riches for any middle-age gay man, but Devon had more on his mind. Sure, he wanted to watch them get off, but he already knew what would follow.

The three friends started fondling themselves. Their erections were taut, and Devon admired them as he encouraged the guys to work on their wood. The tall stud was doing long, firm strokes, while his blond buddy did short, purposeful pulls. The third, an Hispanic hunk with a good amount of curly chest hair, already had pre-cum flowing.

"You guys ever suck one another?" Devon knew how to get the results he wanted. Blondie knelt in the sand and put the tall guy's cock to his lips. Devon looked at the remaining guy and silently commanded him to fill the other's open mouth. Soon the three were licking and sucking in unison. Devon looked on as the buddies serviced one another. Their firm cocks moved in and out of their mouths with ease, and Devon felt their desires rising along with his own needs. *Better speed this along,* he thought. *I need my dinner.*

The tall dude was now pumping his cock into the Latin dude's handsome face. Devon silently came up behind and started licking his neck. "It's OK," he whispered. The tall guy sped up his face-fucking. "Don't pull out," Devon instructed. The cocksucker nodded his agreement. His own dick was pistoning into Blondie, who was frantically jerking. "Let's do it, guys," Devon directed, and with that, the guys started simultaneously shooting. Jizz was propelled deep into both throats, while the blond guy's seed drenched the sand. Devon watched with satisfaction as the students emptied their full sacs.

In a daze, each boy nodded off in post-orgasm bliss. This was the moment Devon had waited for. All the prep work was done. Now he could feast. Devon looked around the deserted beach. The flames flicked at the three naked bodies in front of him. His desire could no longer be contained. As the full moon cast shadows on his timeless face, Devon's fangs descended. It was time for him to be nourished by their youthful blood.

As usual, Tommy's day started with calisthenics. He did his sit-ups and push-ups before hitting the shower. He had an early class, then back to canvassing—if the weather allowed. He looked out his bedroom window to see some rare gray skies. The TV was still blaring with reports of that tropical storm, but Tommy was dedicated to his mission. He also wanted to cruise the parking lot of The Palm later, so he was hopeful as he got dressed for school.

Devon woke up feeling rejuvenated. The infusion from the three young studs had replenished his will. He was even feeling a bit hopeful as he looked out at the clouds. *At least we've a respite from the eternal sunshine,* he thought as he perused the newspaper. He was considering his plans for the afternoon as the TV warned of more wind and rain on the way. *Oh, good.*

Tommy was picking up a fresh batch of pamphlets from the local copy shop. He was planning to meet Ted to finish up where they'd left off on Monday. But as he waited at the counter, he got a text from his brother. Ted was stuck at work and couldn't join him. *Damn.* Tommy knew he wasn't supposed to go out alone, but he wanted to finish that last block. It was on his way home. "Maybe I'll just swing by…"

The street was empty as Devon looked out the front window. He was debating whether to drive into town before the storm hit. It was almost dark outside, so he knew it was safe. As he let the curtain fall, he caught a glimpse of a figure at the end of the block. He squinted. It was the blond twink he was lusting after just yesterday.

Devon smoothed his hair. *Maybe he'll ring again.* The wind was howling outside as he sipped some black coffee. The bell rang. He stood quickly and walked to the door. He peeked outside and saw a vision in blond. He gently opened the door and smiled.

"Yes?"

Tommy was surprised someone had actually answered. "Hello, sir, I'm Tommy. My brother and I left you some reading material yesterday. I was wondering …"

His words trailed off as he got a good look at Devon, who was dressed in leather pants and a tight red shirt. Tommy often fantasized about attractive older men, and now one was standing in front of him. As for Devon, he was only thinking about how to get Tommy inside.

"Yes, I did," he said. "Thank you. I'm Devon …"

He extended a hand to shake, and Tommy couldn't help but notice the red-stoned ring on his finger. "Do you have a minute to talk?"

"Of course. May I invite you in? It's looking rather nasty out there."

"Yeah, it's very windy," Tommy replied. He wasn't supposed to go into a stranger's house alone. This was strictly against the rules.

But he sensed the older man was somehow trustworthy. Plus, it was starting to rain. "Um, I guess it's OK," he said, as Devon held the door open.

The living room curtains were drawn, so Devon turned on a table lamp. The room was still slightly shadowed, but he liked it that way.

Tommy sat back on the sofa uneasily. *What was he doing here?* He wasn't sure, but something about the situation excited him. He felt a boner starting to spring in his pants. "Do you have the pamphlet we left you?" he asked.

"I do. It's right here." Devon went into the kitchen and reached into the recyclable bin. The piece was right on top.

"You can see from the cover that we have a special story this month about …"

Just then there was a loud clap of thunder and a crash from outside. Tommy jumped in his seat. Devon put his hand on the young man's knee to soothe him, and he couldn't help but notice the bulge in Tommy's trousers. Then the room went completely dark. Devon went to the window and threw open the curtains. He could see smoke rising in the distance.

"Looks like a transformer was hit by lightning," he said matter-of-factly. Tommy had come up beside him. Together, they watched as nature put on a showstopper of light and sound. Tommy could smell Devon's musky cologne, and it took all his courage to slip his arm around Devon's trim waist.

Devon continued staring straight ahead and thought, *Maybe there's a God after all.* He casually placed his arm around Tommy's shoulder. Next thing Tommy knew, he was catapulted to the couch.

"Whoa, what just happened?"

Devon smiled. "Let's get comfortable till the power comes back." He quickly lit some candles, then sat next to Tommy.

This sure beats the parking lot of The Palm, Tommy thought. He decided to seize this opportunity. "Can I ask you something?" he said as he pulled himself up.

Devon nodded.

"Have you sucked a lot of guys?"

Devon chuckled, pleased with the direction of the conversation. "A few."

"Well, how can you tell when they're going to … you know …" Tommy paused with embarrassment.

"Oh, you will know. Trust me," Devon said.

Tommy had been thinking about being sucked for a long time. Devon might be his one chance.

"Unzip your pants," Devon said, almost reading Tommy's mind. He had tasted teen blood just last night, but now he was thinking of tasting something else.

Tommy stood up and undid the top button of his pants. Slowly he let his zipper come down. He was wearing his favorite pair of striped boxers and his erection was straining at the waistband. Tommy stood in front of Devon, who was still seated on the couch. Devon drank in the sight of the young man, then reached up and started kneading the hard-on through the cloth.

"Take it out," Devon directed. By this point, Tommy couldn't imagine not taking it out. His dick sprang up as soon as it was freed, and Devon admired the ring of light blond pubes surrounding it. And then it dawned on him who Tommy reminded him of. It was his maker—the blond twink who had turned him into a vampire and eventually lured him to Florida. It had been years ago, and Devon rarely thought of him. But Tommy's tight body and perfect cock brought back the memory.

"See, it's easy to tell when a guy is turned on," Devon said.

Tommy sighed. The thought of the older man sucking him made

him shudder with excitement. Without waiting, he plunged his dick into the warmth and wetness of Devon's mouth.

Devon, who usually had a taste for blood, now had a taste for jizz. He started slowly, though, knowing he had to be careful or this young gun might shoot. He started licking under the cock head and was rewarded with a bead of pre-cum. The sweetness of it sent a bolt of electricity through Devon, who then worked up and down the shaft, nibbling the head.

Tommy's eyes rolled back. By the time Devon went deep-throat, he was panting. "Oh God, oh God," Tommy moaned.

And with that, Devon started sucking deeper, keeping his mouth tight around the nubile rod. Tommy could feel the suction of Devon's full lips. When he noticed himself exhaling long, deep breaths, he knew he was going to pop. He tried to indicate this to Devon, but Devon just nodded. He knew what was next. As he felt the first hot blast of Tommy's sweet cum hit the back of his mouth, he started swallowing. There was a lot, and it coated his throat. When Tommy opened his eyes, he was smiling.

"And that's how you know," Devon said. He waited a moment for Tommy to catch his breath then got right to the point. "So … have you ever been fucked?"

Tommy was slow to answer, but he figured he might as well be honest.

"No, but I do think about it … all the time! What's it like?"

"It can be an intense bonding experience," Devon said.

Tommy suddenly noticed he was still wearing his tie! "Get undressed," Devon said as he undid his own leather pants. Tommy awkwardly stepped out of his clothes and watched as Devon pulled out his own piece. He almost gasped at the size.

"Lie down," Devon said, as Tommy moved to the couch. He felt Devon come up behind him. He could feel Devon's bare skin next to his. Tommy had been thinking about this for a long time, and now, thanks to an act of nature (and God, perhaps?), it was happening. Lying naked together felt good to him. And when Devon leaned in to kiss him, that felt even better. Tommy let his hand roam downward to Devon's hard cock. It was thick and felt meaty in his palm. Devon reached around and started playing with Tommy's tight hole. At first it resisted but once the youth relaxed, it opened for him. First for his fingers and then ...

Tommy felt Devon entering him. Devon held Tommy close as he invaded his virgin ass. The entry was slow but smooth. He was inches from Tommy's neck, but blood was not what Devon desired. He wanted to possess the boy's butt. And fucking it was the best way to do that.

Tommy felt himself becoming rock-hard again. His cock started throbbing as his ass was being penetrated for the first time. Devon had years of experience opening up a bottom, and soon he had Tommy groaning with pleasure. Devon gently flipped him over so he could pound Tommy face-to-face. Before long Devon felt himself nearing orgasm. He pulled out of Tommy and aimed at his smooth chest. Tommy's eyes were glued to Devon's cock as it began spouting warm juice all over him.

"Oh, yes—oh, yes!" was all Tommy could muster before he shot more of his own copious cum. Moments later, the pair was entangled in a messy heap.

Outside, the storm was passing. Tommy relaxed into Devon's arms and fell snugly asleep. Devon looked down at the boy. He was so innocent and peaceful. He breathed deep into Tommy's tousled hair. He let him rest for a while, then nudged him.

"It's getting late," Devon whispered.

Tommy bolted awake. "Oh, no! My parents will be worried!" He looked at his phone, which displayed numerous texts. "I better get going." Tommy started grabbing his clothes. Devon looked on with a bemused expression. The boy was so young and so cute. Sure, Devon had had the opportunity to drain more than Tommy's cum while he dozed, but he'd resisted feeding on the young man. "Though he would make an ideal companion …" he thought.

"Thanks for saving me from the storm," Tommy said as he buttoned his shirt.

"My pleasure," Devon answered.

Tommy finished tying his shoes and reached into his bag. "Hey, here's another pamphlet for you," Tommy said. "Maybe I can come back and we can discuss it sometime?"

Devon nodded. "I would like that."

He watched as Tommy left and walked briskly down the dark, damp street. At first, he felt a rush of disappointment. He was alone again, an ageless bloodsucker stranded in Florida, his maker long lost to the one true death. But then he stopped and looked at the flyer in his hand and the cover headline made him laugh out loud: ETERNAL LIFE OR ETERNAL STRIFE? YOU DECIDE!

SWARM

Chip Masterson

Sturges woke this morning by nuzzling against my neck and rubbing his turgid gut-puncher against my thigh. My fingers fumbled down and hesitantly grasped the cool, thick-veined organ, not wanting to set it off prematurely—not in my hand at least. I rolled over him and trapped it between my thighs, frottaging its shrouded head against the thin membrane cording my boys to my taint, swabbing some spit down with my other hand to keep his idling core-driller slick.

Sturges trapped my cock against my abs with his palm, kneading it like a spent tube of toothpaste, raising its fullness with alternating pressures. He disliked kissing, so I stuck my nose in his ear, slowly exhaling.

I twisted around to straddle his torso, gently massaging loose muscles developed through years of hard labor, as alien to me as his existence is to mine. I stroked his armpits and dug my fingers under his ribbed musculature, leaning forward and spreading my cheeks in invitation. Rising like a boa tasting the air, his grease monkey tickled my hungry hole and pushed through, spelunking for hemoglobin.

I settled back, letting him slither in as my weight caressed him, caught him in a muscular embrace and twisted ever so slightly back and forth as I released him bit by bit. His fingernails grazed the insides of my thigh and brushed against my aching dick as his hips bucked me like a stud sliding into skinny jeans. We worked into a rhythm; I pressed down on his chest in sync with my own breath and captured his cold tongue between my wet lips, sucking it into my hot mouth.

Sturges began surging his groin into my ass as he grasped my tongue with this teeth and pulled me back—then sank down while lifting his shoulders, writhing and coiling his arms around me. The beat sped up as he rode me from below and, releasing my tongue, drew in a sharp breath as he prepared to feed.

His rigid shaft gripped my borehole with needle-like fibers that pierced his skin and sunk into my flesh. Drawing my pulsations into himself through this stud-siphon, his grinding loins grew warmer, the gray skin fattening pinkly, the glow spreading through him as my heart pumped blood through his dead arteries and pulled it back through his withering veins. His entire body became a blazing erection, engorged with my energizing life-stream refreshing and arresting the decay that gripped his dead limbs. Every cell of Sturges's body sang for the blood, yearning for the sustenance only fresh human blood could provide, delaying the inevitable putrefaction a little while longer.

I splooged several pearlescent strands upon the rocky soil of his abs and chest, falling forward to squeeze it between us and smear our bodies as if it could glue us together—my life enough to sustain us both forever. I knew that could never be, but the flush of heat flowing through him matched the spurting hotness from my balls, and for a moment we were a single beast with one heart.

And then I fell back asleep.

Sturges was dabbing blood on his flaking ankle when I woke again. Looking for my skivvies, I caught his reflection in a hanging machete and shrieked. I lay back until the spinning nausea passed.

Sturges strained his ear into the quiet and said, "I don't hear anything. What—?" He stopped, saw the unsheathed blade, and scowled at me. "That's why we put things away. Everything tidy."

The Zombie Apocalypse really fucked the vampires. Vampires aren't really sexy. They're mobile corpses. Feeding only arrests decay—it can't reverse it. You see a saggy-skinned skull creak toward you, sunken eyes jittery with interest, and you hear the scrape of dry tendons over worn bones as a dead arm sweeps that dusty sweet-pungent stank—and your brain goes into shock, refusing it. A vampire mentally grasps that moment and reassures you, "No, I'm young and hot," and you gratefully agree and see it whole, lusting, with blood pressure. Your mind rehinges itself, and that horniness that follows grief raises its stake for life itself—and your risen stake leads you in the illusion.

Zombies fucked that. The only human survivors adapted to shambling corpse-hordes quickly, seeing the dead for what they were, and vampires lost their leverage. Now we see the predatory corpse, but with scary intelligence. In the beginning, it got ugly—but in the end, we formed a symbiotic partnership: Vampires can fight zombies, which only want warm flesh. And our dwindling feed our protectors. Feudalism reborn.

A commotion sounded down the tunnel, a subway line long out of service. All the surface entries had been blocked, but zombies get sucked into underground rivers and bob back up right in your lap. Nasty and gnashing.

The stampede clamored into view, most vampires carrying humans and others hanging back. The fighters slung the wet things onto the third rail. (Thank God the generator got fixed. Unlike in most stories, zombies and vampires aren't vulnerable in their brains or hearts. Each individual cell is "reanimated"—detached, meaning it might dry up but it won't "die" die. The being is really a swarm of mindless cells, like bees or locusts; vampires retain some brain-intelligence whereas brain-dead zombies only alight, devour, move on. Only immolation stops them for good, but a strong charge can fry one stiff for a spell.)

Sturges hauled me over his shoulder and entered the scrum, exchanging pleasantries with friends. "Yeah, all Gators," Boswick confirmed. "Real bloaty—musta jammed up at a bend or something."

The all-clear party signaled a safe tunnel by flickering their lights. We piled through the heavy door into the downward-sloping tunnel. Someday the warren would be overrun. For now, we wove the labyrinthine dark with humans' fogged breath. My ears popped as we crossed the portal into a station—191st Street. It smelled salty—the ocean table steadily rising.

I shivered but not just from the cold. The IRT into Jersey had flooded; pumping made it passable, but not secure. Zombies can wait like eels in the mud until warm meat wakes them. Meat, they want; blood, they waste. Strange.

"Look what we got!" someone yelled. A circle opened on the platform and we saw it—a zombie in full rigor mortis. It was Johnny—a wasted heroin needle with a schlong big as my forearm. Now it rose straight out through his ragged jeans, no doubt harder than it ever got in life.

Cheers and jeers split the crowd and a vampire led his human to the corpse. "This is your big chance, Fido," the VP said. The meat's eyes glittered.

"Oh, no," I grimaced, turning away. I don't care how many condoms I'm wearing, I'm not going to risk a tear. A single hungry zombie cell can turn the Staff of Life necrotic overnight, and you're done for.

The VP was unrolling a series of extra-large condoms onto Johnny's main mast and then circling it with Saran Wrap and lube. He picked up his feverish pervert and set him on it, letting the human's flesh be gravity's bitch for a change. I thought of an old video with an orange highway cone and winced.

Security stood by with a blowtorch and lighter fluid: If the perv comes into contact with the zombie in any way, they'll both be sent up. The vampire stopped the impalement with several inches to go when the guy slimed the crowd with spunk. The vampire wrenched his human off so fast he shrieked; tension ratcheted up while Security checked the blood-slicked stalagcock for any breaks. "It's clean," he announced, ironically.

The perv was carried away, head lolling back deliriously from the rushing danger. Johnny began to list, the rigor releasing him, as Security dragged him with a hook into an elevator shaft and lit him up.

Speaking of rigor, I was hard again, so I turned my potent vitality on Sturges with a rage for conquest. I grabbed him roughly, pressed him into the tile, and ripped his pants down. I rammed myself into his sadly loose interior. "Can't you tighten anything?"

"Give it a sec," he muttered—and then his butt muscle strangled me and a thousand shards of glass plunged into my bone, practically sucking me up and off my feet. "Jesus Fuckhole Cunting Christ!"

Endorphins flooded my meatprobe and electrified me with a whole-body orgasmic revelation. The clamping pressure pulsed me, drawing my pecker-spit but holding it back, his innards contorting me like a hundred Krav Maga-trained acrobat-whores. I let his power-guts drag me into the air as I frantically, yet carefully, clutched and squeezed his back, arms, and shoulders. I finally shot piercingly rapturous juice into him, then fell limp and moaned sickly from my second bleeding; he broke out of his crapulence and, with effort, shat me out.

I must have passed out. When I shivered myself awake, he was still standing there, immobile. I grabbed his leg to pull myself up, its rigidity comforting and arousing. His head swiveled back and forth and he looked down. "Here we are."

We crept slowly back to the platform and peered around the corner. I stepped out into the vast open space and shivered, riven with panic and a childish feeling of being left behind. "Where'd everyone go?"

"Who do mean?" Demir asked. I focused and looked from side to side.

"Here we are," I said, and blinked. *Didn't Sturges just say that?*

I saw Demir—we were sitting in a kiosk under Bleecker Street.

I am Sturges.

There is no symbiotic truce. Humans fight us. There is only fighting. Fighting and hunger.

"You were away for a long time," Demir said. "I started to wonder if you were coming back."

"I'm glad I did," I murmured. He approached, a wide-shouldered silhouette, his manly amplitude bouncing back and forth on his thighs beneath loose khakis like a bell clapper. I trapped them against one with my face and pressed it, shoving my nose in and sucking the side of his Cyclops through the cotton. He pulled my head tighter and undid his pants, shucking them down to his knees, proud of a fullness even death could not defeat. I slid my tongue around the glans beneath the sheath, stretching it slightly and rolling it back so I could suckle the full tip and tongue his slit.

Demir's rough thumb pulled my jaw down and I swallowed the firehose as he turned the pressure on. Most of his remaining plasma pushed into his porkroll and it moved in my throat as if alive, seeking heat, pulse, life. I closed my lips and teeth gingerly around the base to keep the blood from ebbing away from my cold cavity and pressed my tongue into his vein. He moaned and I stuck my fingers into his

134

he-pussy, stretching and stirring the dull nerves. He shivered as a dry heave hitched his stones in vestigial orgasm, his nerves briefly fluttering with empty pleasure.

I kept him in me until he pried my mouth open and slipped his rapidly deflating feeding tube away. I looked up and he smiled, a little sadly, but very happily.

He plopped next to me and sighed. "We need to eat." I snuggled under his big still-hairy arm. Demir was much younger—there was more of him left, tattoos still whole. "I think I remember hearing about a Colonial-era Hellfire Club not far from here. Near Wall Street—maybe some hungry survivors are making food raids from all those sealed vaults."

We headed south, hand in hand, watchfully. "At the beginning," I said, gathering as best I could the now-scattering memories of my away time, "I—I was human," I said, puzzled. "I found an old Victrola. Spun a warped record, filling the dark with Ethel Merman and Bert Lahr singing 'Friendship' onstage somewhere."

"I don't know what any of those things are," said Demir, who had been barely out of his teens when the world died.

"Doesn't matter—point is, it's a funny song by two old stage hams. The crowd is eating them up, laughter surging between verses, meaning Lahr was doing something hysterically funny, which we'll never see. And I—I felt this wrenching in my guts: people dressed up, eating in restaurants, taking taxies and the subway to a big dark auditorium, laughing together with strangers at beloved comedians. Sitting there, perfectly safe. Having fun. It pierced me."

"Huh," Demir commented. "I don't know what to say."

"Just keep fucking me," I said, pressing against him. Without blood pressure, it wasn't feeding—it was almost like real sex.

I recognized where we were. "It was under the courthouse, I think. Close." Plywood panels had once blocked the way, but they'd already been clawed apart. It didn't completely register, the fact that whoever had been going the other way, out of the boarded-up space, that it might mean something. I only thought of that later.

Glow-sticks lit the vaulted room like a sickly rave. I don't know what I'd been expecting—wigs, stocks—but the space was empty. Some graffiti of Alexander Hamilton screwing Aaron Burr while shoving some kind of dildo down General Washington's throat decorated the wall—was that the evidence of what this was? Demir nudged me—there was moaning from another room.

Inside were half a dozen men, barely alive or sane, chained to the walls. We had no idea whose pantry this might be but were too ravenous to care. Demir wheel-barrowed a large man and split the scabrous ass, while I socketed my wrench down his toothless maw. "It's like that scene in *Lady and the Tramp*," I said, grinning.

Again, casting seeds among stones—but Demir had already blissed out, and I felt the first wave of satisfaction spread through me like a stain.

We'd pretty much tapped him out by the time we pulled away. I heard shuffling in the main room, so I, the elder, went first, explaining, "He was about to go south as it is." Then I froze in my tracks.

He—it—stood stock still, fingers tented and head cocked, like some old movie villain. Ming the Merciless. I stepped forward casually and said, "We were starving. We'll find you another one."

"There aren't any more," he replied. He still hadn't moved and I thought of a praying mantis. "Fires have gutted every tower and parking shack. Snow drifts cover shattered glass, wrecks, barricades, explosion debris. Streets are impassable, clotted with trash and charred masonry."

"Well, we'll go upstate, or down the shore. There's got to be pockets of—"

"It doesn't matter. They're not for me." He chucked his chin at the other room.

Demir and I looked at each other. This guy didn't add up, and he looked wrong—his exposed skin … rippled. Quivered. We don't spend that much energy on small effects.

"What's wrong with you?" Demir asked right out.

He didn't smile, and with a stab of foreboding, I realized what he meant. They were for us. They were bait, those wasted, drugged humans.

"I don't know if I'd call it wrong," he responded. "It's interesting."

"It's alarming," I corrected. "Cut the shit—what are you?" As long as we were jumping in feet first.

"I had been hunting out of a nest in Grand Central Station. I hadn't fed in a long time and I sat on the track to rest and went away. When I came back, two throngs of zombies crowded past me—one going north, the other going west. They buffeted past me, bits of them falling on my head and into my mouth, down my neck, into my pants. Had been for some time—I was coated with zombits. I got clear but I'd already started changing. My starved cells consumed parts of the zombie cells and—it worked. With the world rapidly losing food sources, I can absorb the new, growing resource: the reanimated dead.

"It itched at first, and I felt funny, nauseous. I stumbled around a pharmacy, looking for anything might work. I ran into a boy I'd known ages ago. We shook hands out of habit—and my fingers tugged into his cold, dry jerky and … became part of him. He tore off his own arm in panic and fled to get away. And I held it and watched it melt bizarrely into my own arm. His marrow hit me in a rush, and that arm—this arm—became supple.

"After that, I focused on zombies. They never fought back. I felt bigger, fuller, stronger—preserved, rot banished. I think … some cells may be regenerating—restitching into a single organism. Actually approaching life."

I had leaned against Demir and he put his arm around my shoulders, taking my feathery weight. I should have felt relieved—the bait being for them, not us—but I didn't. "What's it feel like—all that … rot?" I asked.

"Retsina—underforest skunkwood notes, plus spicy mildew with a tangy, metallic bite, like yak yoghurt flavored with saffron and durian."

"You must have been in sales," Demir said flatly.

"Aren't you two *lively?*" His eyes glittered.

"We've just fed," Demir growled, lowering his brow and clenching his fists.

"Fight? You want to fight me?" the stranger chuckled. "How? There are no weapons here. Hit me and the swarm is upon you. Care to take a swipe and see?"

"Our skin does let go," I grumbled, turning and hiking up my jeans to show the raw muscle of my calf.

"Not much of a fight though," tisked the stranger, leaning against the door frame. "Flight, more like. To where? Chasing the desperate human remnant into the fermenting tropics?"

Demir eyed him sourly. "I'm not sure I like you. But I gotta know. Do you get—feel—*know*—anything from the zombie's former—?"

The stranger waved his hand. "There's nothing left. Darkness and hunger, that's all." He stood up straight. "Be honest, I'm fuckin' horny," the stranger grinned. "And not brittle anymore. Feeling strong."

Demir squinted through the colonial gloom. "You weren't bad looking once," he surmised with a sigh. "Some Turk would be an improvement." Prick was horny, too.

I stared at Demir. "Are you serious?"

"He's right. Where will we go? What will be left when we get there?

Once the muscle wastes away, we fall into a heap of bones, slowly moldering, locked inside pain and lunacy. If I have to go, I want to go out cumming." He smirked at the poor joke and knelt, unzipping the stranger's fly on the way down. Through the wool trousers, Demir squeezed the bulge appreciatively. "Bigger, too?"

The stranger pulled Demir up by his armpits—no flesh contact—and pressed their crotches together, working Demir's button-fly open. The stranger's package uncoiled like a tentacle, furtively swirled the air, then dove straight into Demir's jeans and, under the denim, vined around his bowsprit. Their bodies jerked together and Demir shuddered, eyes ablaze.

Jealously, I planted my mouth on the stranger's face, squawking as it tugged at me. I dug my fingers into Demir's wrestler's physique and the stranger's pulsating back. Our teeth clicked and bit, my face not twisting to the side but meeting his straight on, nose-to-nose, eye-to-eye, and followed the deep promise I saw there.

I rotated around his head and, shucking my tatters, pulled his trousers down and stuffed myself into his firm, high ass. Our cheeks welded together and his bunghole sucked me, my instinctual hooks being pulled out by their roots and suffused with something more satisfying than blood. A high buzzing warbled in my ears, urging me to press myself into his back, rip away the clothing and join myself with his virility.

Demir tore off his shirt and wherever the stranger's hand roamed, my Turk's skin rippled and seemed to reach up toward it, like iron filings to a magnet. But their skin didn't meld until they grasped fingers and the stranger pulled Demir's hands over his head, backing him against the wall and almost zipping into him, shivering with pleasure.

"Are you absorbing us?" Demir muttered, voice trembling with confusion.

"No—I'm expanding—don't you feel your mind reaching out? I think we're becoming something entirely new," the stranger marveled. Our bodies stretched and welded into each other's, searing heat filling the stale space with the smell of burnt hair and sizzling fat. For one moment our cocks rose out of a single shimmering crotch, a single-rooted, three-headed Cerberus. Overwhelmed with the spirit-bursting release of the union, gobs of fizzing, seething jizz erupted from three gaping mouths. Demir's foreskin spread like a cape and enveloped all three heads, compressing them into a single bobble-globed mushroom. It jetted out one last triumphant arc of steaming cum. Our combined girth bent drippingly down: heavy, frightening, and tempting.

None of us had ever heard of vampires making sperm. An unbearable pressure in our/my head broke and sprayed stars inside me—and I knew what it had been to be Demir, to be Carver.

"What an appropriate name you had," I said—but it wasn't my voice. It wasn't me saying it. A tripartite chord slowly resolved and became a new sound in a new key.

We patched each other up and, with a belching jolt, we felt our massive heart pump. We reeled with the pulse rushing into our tingling limbs. Nothing happened. We inflated our lungs, the stale crud-filled air scraping our throat but that had no real effect. Then, a minute or so later, our heart burped again.

"It seems we'll still be cold-blooded, but with some minimal circulatory system," we said.

I couldn't tell which of our minds might have deduced this—our personalities spun like a kaleidoscope into a single new identity, one with all of our parts and histories but a single will. "Carver was the pupal stage," we said. "We are the Death's-head Moth."

"The Moth-man," I said, chuckling. I sat, having never faced a fully-living meal before. Could I be omnivorous? I wasn't hungry, but

I was randy as *fuck*—and aware the humans stared at me in awe … as at God.

Pump. A cold ichorous sensation creeped through me. I felt glowingly, chillingly alive. Striding over the captives, my fingers easily popped the links that bound them—their hands glommed onto my thighs, my ass cheeks, while emaciated arms pulled bodies upright by grasping the solid branch of my Godcock. Two young men peeled back the leathery hood and began sharing my salt-glistened tenderness while another rubbed his head through my low-slinging nut sac. I had grown too massive for any of them, though one sex pig made an impressive effort of accepting my glans into his cavernous man cunt before his own orgasm racked him so severely I feared he'd herniate himself. I gently lifted him off, and the six of them pressed around my lance, assembling a casing of ardent flesh that I could thrust through while they wrestled and grappled my flesh with all their famished strength and hunger.

I pressed my hands against the ceiling of the small cell. One began dandling my taint and pulling on it, opening my hole but only blowing inside. I grunted, repressing the first surge, and felt the stone above me crack and shift. Dust and gravel sifted down onto the orgiasts who redoubled their efforts, squeezing their bodies together to choke me within their bear-hugging embrace. I roared as the first spritz of my viscous protein shake splattered against the far wall. I shoved my arms up, shattering rock and concrete exploding into the subway tunnel above. Ties splintered and the rails squealed and wrenched apart.

I stuck my arms through the hole and hauled myself off the ground while my worshippers pummeled the base of my virility and swung like apes from my twisting junk. My bellows rocketed through the tunnel as I drenched the revelers in literally gallons of precious protein which they hungrily scraped and licked into their mouths. I had a dim sense it might actually be nutritious to them.

Zombies shuffled down the tunnel toward me, their dead eyes shadowed by the few slivers of light streaming from shafts above us. I was hungry: hungry for these mutants. I wanted to consume them wholly, flesh into flesh, and convert what strange energy animates them into new life for me, with my excretion nourishing my new pets.

I wondered briefly if there might be others like me, evolving from hunted, starved refugees into vibrant cell-conscious new creatures. As if this all had been building to this ultimate Darwinian triumph. A resurrection of the flesh, by the flesh, in the flesh and for the flesh. A myth of deity being born in real time, real space, with no false promises, tests, or burdens. Only absorbing and fucking. And spreading. Swarming.

Alive.

MOVIE MONSTER MAYHEM!

Landon Dixon

I was pounding out another pulp western on my battered old Underwood when Ted Pine burst into my Ivor Street apartment and exclaimed, "I'm making a movie! And I want *you* to write the script!"

The smile blazing across Ted's boyishly handsome face had more juice in it than a Klieg light, and his doe-brown eyes twinkled like the stars over Hollywood. I sighed and looked back down at the half-sheet of horse opera I'd already embroidered. "Uh-huh."

The only thing overarching Ted Pine's enthusiasm for filmmaking was his inability to get movies made. He had more story tunes than a one-man band, less actual produced work than a Tin Pan Alley cat. "This time, it's for real!" he exulted, clapping me on the shoulders. "I've got the film, the cameras, the crew, and a pair of fresh foreign faces that will absolutely, positively electrify the horror genre! Guaranteed!"

I was two months behind on the rent and desperate to place at least one oater with the pulpwood markets before they rode off into the sunset for good. "Have you got the financing?" I grumbled.

Ted glanced down at me from his head up in the celluloid clouds. "Yes!" he announced, shocking me into attention. "Five thousand dollars in the bank! All I need is a script!"

"That never stopped you before …"

Ted swept the air with his hands, like a magician about to mesmerize an audience before a con. "This is a new era, Phil! The 1950s! And I'm going to lead a horror movie revival, the likes of which hasn't been seen since the Universal monsters of the thirties and forties!"

I'd had the misfortune of scripting a couple of Ted Pine's previous C pictures, and now I was his go-to scribe. And Ted was a force of ballyhoo nature virtually impossible to resist. He grinned at me, arms outstretched, mouth and ears wide open and waiting. "OK," I groaned. "What's the flick about? And who are the 'stars'?"

Ted's teeth and eyes flashed more wattage. "It's … a vampire film! And the stars … Oh boy, the stars! Let me introduce you!"

He rushed for the door, flung it open. "Meet Boris Leturno and Karl Belgrade—the best of Balkans' cinema!"

They stood in my apartment doorway, both clad entirely in black—suits, ties, shoes, and socks—their faces and hands so pale by contrast they just about glowed.

"Come in, boys!" Ted directed. "Meet your scriptwriter—the prominent pulp, comic book, and silver screen scenarist, Phil Foster!"

The pair entered. I stood up and shook their hands. Their clasps were as cool as the smiles on their faces. Boris was tall and slender and distinguished-looking, with dark hair silvered at the temples and swept back in a widow's peak, a broad face, red lips and rather heavy brow, elegant manners. Karl was shorter and stockier, but just as aristocratic-appearing, with slick black hair and a tall forehead, dark eyes and long nose and square jaw, large hands, equally elegant manner. They both bowed as they took and shook my hand.

"Beautiful, aren't they!?" Ted expounded. "And fine actors! Sensa-

144

tions of the Romanian stage and screen, here to conquer Hollywood!" He gripped my arm and lowered his tone about fifty decibels, adding for my ears only, "I don't *think* we'll have to dub their voices."

I looked dubious, spoke same. "What kind of vampire pic did you have in—"

"Something chilling and charming, if you please. And—"

"Cheap," I finished the tagline on every Pine production.

"Don't, uh, forget to put in some cross-dressing, too, OK?" Ted's personal and professional peccadillo, along with his penchant for stock footage and one-takes.

Gripping Boris and Karl by the shoulders, he hustled them out of my dingy apartment. "We're off to Schwab's! To lunch, gentlemen, to lunch!"

I delivered the completed shooting script to Ted's cubbyhole office over a bowling alley on Cahuenga six days later. I'd put an extra effort into this one, with the prospect of actually being paid.

"Ah! *Fangs for Francie, Bangs for Bobby*!" Ted read, leaping out of the wobbly wooden chair behind his bill-strewn desk. "I love it! We begin shooting tonight!"

"Sure, Phil. But let me give you a synopsis of—"

"I'll read it on-set! You tell it to Boris and Karl! I have to check on a studio!" He barged out of the room and raced down the hall.

Boris and Karl strolled into the office from the adjoining john. I went over the script with the pair. "Basically, it's a boy-loves-girl, girl-is-bitten-by-a-vampire-and-becomes-undead, boy-still-loves-girl-so-dresses-up-as-a-girl-to-entice-vampires-to-bite-him-so-he-can-still-love-girl-in-undead-form story," I summarized.

They nodded, sitting in chairs on either side of me, Boris on my left, Karl on my right. The tattered green blind was pulled down on the flyblown one window, creating a twilight effect. I could feel more of the pair's charm, sitting so close, their thighs and shoulders pressing into mine. I also felt a slight buzzing in my head and a sudden drowsiness in my bones, the air becoming heavy.

"So, uh, Bobby's so infected with love for Francie that he's even willing to take the big bite, to be with his lover ... on the other side."

"I understand perfectly," Boris intoned, placing a slim, cool hand on my thigh.

"Brilliant," Karl murmured gravely, placing a big, cool hand on my other thigh.

I gulped, my vision blurring, the air thick as cobwebs now. I could barely breathe. They had a way about them, an old-country, cunning, sensuous way. My cock started expanding in my pants, engorging with blood. They sensed it, their eyes glittering and lips shining and nostrils flaring with feeling, hands rubbing my thighs higher and higher.

"B-But the vampires—you two—w-won't bite Bobby, grant him his wish, at first. Because he's a boy. S-So, he puts on some of Francie's clothes—her pink angora sweater and polka dot poodle skirt and black pumps. And Bobby goes walking in the park at night. And-And the vampires see him, and think he's a she and swoop down and b-bite him ... her."

Boris and Karl clutched my thighs up near my surging groin, their fingers digging erotically into my flesh, though with no actual warmth. My cock rose rigid as a coffin lid. I blurted, "And Bobby and Francie live happily ever after, and ever after, and ever after ..."

The pair closed in on me from either side, sandwiching me between them, unable to move. They tilted their heads, opened their mouths. My neck seemed to stretch like my cock, veins throbbing with blood.

"I got the key to the Quality Works soundstage!" Ted yelped, bursting into the office and triumphantly dangling a silver key between his outstretched fingers. "We'll shoot scenes one to twenty-five tonight! The graaaaveyard …!"

Quality Works had been a poverty row studio during the 1930s and forties, and their stock had only declined at the outset of the 1950s. The "soundstage" was little more than a large, dirty room with one end slightly elevated. The "set" was pure Pine-work: cardboard tombstones taped onto green carpet grass—the graveyard. The cast and crew was all-Pine as well, his usual assortment of oddballs and cast-offs that followed him from one discount epic to another like he was a poor man's DeMille.

Gary Glammer was in charge of makeup and wardrobe, was the set designer, gaffer, and best boy. Heinie Weiss was the cameraman and cinematographer. That was the crew.

The cast consisted of: former Irish wrestling sensation-turned-souse Barney Stone, playing the henchman; Farley "Long" Doung, playing a cop; Vella St. Cyr, occupying the role of virginal young Francie, despite her forty years and three abortions; and Ziggy Marcelino, as Bobby, the clean-cut All-American blue-eyed blond-haired boy, despite Ziggy's swarthy looks and extensive juvenile criminal record. And Boris and Karl, as the vampires, of course.

The filming went as well as could be expected on a seat-of-your-pants, out-on-your-ass production. Tombstones wobbled and fell over, Barney tripped and tore a run in the "grass," Vella slapped Long Doung across the face when the hung, horny sixty-year-old whispered a few ad-libbed obscenities in her ear. Ziggy stopped production to smoke up some inspiration in the bathroom, and Heinie shuttered the camera a couple of times until he got the back pay owe him from Ted.

As usual, I wanted to hide my head in a brown paper bag and burn my Writers Guild membership card in shame. But I did keep my eyes peeled and hands free to watch the performances of Boris and Karl.

The pair were good. Their voices chillingly dripped with Transylvanian accents, their movements were fluid and animal-like, their seductive powers translated well on-set like they had back in Ted's office. Ted sat sprawled in his homemade canvas director's chair clutching his bullhorn in one hand and petting his angora sweater with the other, enthralled like the rest of us.

We lensed all through the night and into the early morning. Ted only had the studio for twelve hours, before the County of Los Angeles seized it for back taxes. He had half the script in the can by four a.m. No rehearsals or retakes required.

We wrapped, and the cast and crew departed. I hung around in the washroom, penciling in some changes to the next night's shooting script, seated on the toilet with the screenplay in my lap. Until I heard a noise outside, like somebody ... slurping? Was Ziggy going over his "lines" with a straw?

I zipped up and stepped out, looked towards the graveyard set at the far end of the room. It was Ziggy, all right. Only, the young hustler-turned-actor wasn't going over his lines. He was going over Boris's and Karl's cocks. I had to grab onto the screenplay to keep it from tumbling onto the floor.

Boris and Karl were standing two abreast on the green carpet between a pair of tombstones, their long, hard, pale cocks out and in Ziggy's hands and mouth. The D-list thespian was down on his knees in the graveyard, the back of his curly head to me. He was pulling on Boris's cock, stroking urgently and underhanded; sucking on Karl's cock, blowing tight and rapidly. Then he shifted his head and his handiwork, latching onto and swirling his olive-toned hand up and down Karl's gleaming ivory pole, lipping onto and suctioning his big mouth back and forth on Boris's glistening porcelain pipe.

148

The set was all but dark, just some moonlight shafting in from a broken window up top, illuminating in shimmering silver the pretend graveyard and the very real threesome. The only sound was Ziggy's slurping as he sucked and tugged. Boris and Karl stood stock-still, still dressed in their vampire regalia, towering above Ziggy both vertically and horizontally.

It was eerie, erotic; uncanny and otherworldly.

I looked around. The rest of the room was cloaked in blackness.

I stuffed the script under my arm and my pencil behind my ear, unzipped my pants and pulled my swelling cock out onto the scene. A couple of right-handed jacks and I was as long and hard as Boris and Karl, if a little more florid. Watching the handsome pair get sucked and stroked.

Boris gestured, and Ziggy popped a cock out of his mouth, let go of the other in his hand. He stood up and stripped off his sweater-slacks-loafers teenybopper combination, got down to the skin. Then he went down on his hands and knees in the "grass." He moved rapidly, but methodically, as if entranced by the pair and their pair. I know I was.

The twenty-year-old had a smooth, supple, caramel-colored body, except for a couple of bushy brown thatches at the chest and groin. His cock was clean-cut, thick as a man's forearm. He stuck his well-rounded bottom up into the air, arching his back and raising his head, gripping the carpet on all fours.

Boris lubed his cock, moving into penetrating position behind Ziggy. Karl stepped up in front, his cock looming large in the lad's face. Boris bent at the knees and spread Ziggy's ripe cheeks, speared his cock in between. Karl bent at the knees and plunged his cock in between Ziggy's plush lips while Boris thrust deep into the kid's ass.

The pair grunted, hard cocks sheathed in hot, young man. I gasped and fisted my own dong, staring in awe at the strange, shadow-shrouded sex scene.

The pair fucked Ziggy ass and mouth, grasping his buttocks and head and driving their cocks into his anus and face. The dark, musty air was filled with the animalistic groans of the pair, the slurping sound of Ziggy's throat and chute, the crack of thighs off cheeks and the flap of balls against chin. Plus my own ragged breathing and fapping.

The atmosphere grew heavier, headier, clouds scudding across the moon outside to produce an almost lightning-like effect on the fucking threesome. Ziggy's ass and mouth knew no depths, taking churning cocks to the limit of sexual endurance and enthrallment.

The tension mounted, the barometric pressure dropping, as the pumping cock pressure built and built, dazzling my orbs and thundering in my veins. The air chilled, even as the action heated up.

Until Boris was flinging his cock into Ziggy's ass in a bone-boring, cheek-spanking frenzy, reaming the kid's anus. And then he threw back his head and howled. Just as Karl slammed his cock into Ziggy's mouth and throat in a blur and threw back his head and howled the same. The pair came inside Ziggy, shuddering and shooting, barking at the moon as they blasted the boy.

I bucked and whimpered and lined ropes of white-hot semen out the tip of my hand-cranked cock, paying sticky, striping tribute to the trio of sexsters like it was stag night down at The Gay Gaucho on Fremont. I jerked with each jolting jet, pouring out my appreciation.

But then my hand froze on my hose and my soul went as cold as a publisher's heart. Boris and Karl had pulled out of Ziggy, pushed him down flat on the carpet, pinned him there. And now they were crouched over his outstretched neck on either side, biting and sucking and … feeding, it looked like! Ziggy's laid-out body convulsed, his upthrust cock quivering. The temperature internally and externally plummeted, the wildly stimulating scene gone wickedly ghoulish.

My dick drooped and dribbled, my dry mouth hanging open, my ears now pounding with the sinister sounds of frantic animal sucking and drinking; Boris and Karl attacking their immobilized prey at the neck. And then my eyes almost popped out of my reeling head, my thumping heart stopped, as I saw Ziggy's body buck violently and his rigidly upright cock fountain semen into the air all on its own—burst after brutal, terrifying burst.

I stumbled back into the washroom. I was halfway out the window with my pants still down around my ankles when I heard the new howling. Spine-chilling, blood-curdling baying that I'd never before heard on God's green earth. Horrific cries from below and beyond!

"Phil! Just the talented scribe I wanted to see!" Ted leapt out of his director's chair and tossed his bullhorn aside and rushed over to me.

The location was Griffith Park late at night, the setting the rustic Transylvanian countryside, a tub of dry ice and one single fan providing the fog-seeping atmosphere amongst the dry yellow grass and towering palms of LA. The scene was the one where Boris and Karl confer on their course of action after seeing Bobby strolling around in his fishnets and angora.

I'd tried to stay away after what I'd witnessed (and participated in) the previous night. But something irresistible had drawn me back.

"Boris and Karl are having a bit of trouble with the dialogue you've given them," Ted rolled on, clasping my shoulder with one hand as he showed me the script with the other. "They say it's not quite as authentic as it could be. How about running through their lines with them, huh?"

I looked past Ted, at the cast and crew standing around in the moonlight. Every weirdo one of them was there except Ziggy.

"Ted, I need to talk to you about Boris and Karl," I said in an undertone, dragging him further away from the shoot.

"Well, could you make it snappy? We don't have a permit to film here and there's a patrol car due by in about fifteen minutes." He glanced nervously up at the winding road fifty feet away through the brush.

That explained his unusually subdued tone of voice—he didn't want to rouse any bums and get them bawling to the police.

"Hey, Ted! Barney just passed out cold!" Gary Glammer yelled next to the stretched-out, bloated frame of the Irishman, breaking the relative calm.

"Good! Good!" Ted shouted back, unable to control himself. "It'll add …" he waved a hand theatrically through the air, "atmosphere!"

He gripped my shoulder again. "Now, for Pete's sake, Phil, what is it? You act like you've seen a ghost."

"Not ghosts. Ted, I'm pretty sure Boris and Karl are really …"

"Yes!?"

"I think they're actually *vampires!*"

"They *are* vampires! That's the whole point of the pic—"

"No! Vampires in real life! Or unreal death, or half-life—whatever they call it. Honest-to-badness *real* vampires!"

Ted stared at me, the moonlight shining off the brilliantine in his brown hair. Then his fingers dug into my flesh, and his eyes all but pinwheeled. "Say! That's a swell idea, Phil! I can sell the movie that way!"

He gestured with both hands, lost again in his delusions of cinematic grandeur. "Two unknowns, cast straight out of Romania! They play vampires, perhaps … too well! Because maybe, just maybe … they *are* vampires! No acting required!"

"Ted! I saw them with Ziggy last—"

But there was no stopping—or talking to—Ted once he got an idea and the publicity campaign started rolling. He rushed back to his director's chair and started scribbling away on his script, no doubt composing a press release avec purple prose.

152

Boris and Karl walked solemnly over, took me by the arms, and led me into the pitch-black-painted Airstream trailer that served as their on-location dressing rooms and parking lot dwelling quarters. The interior was lit by a single candle sitting on a dark wood table. The pair seated me on the red velvet couch facing the table and candle, then sat down next to me on either side.

"We need to discuss your ... vision," Boris breathed in my ear on the right.

"Discover what you had in mind for us," Karl breathed in my ear on the left.

I gulped. There wasn't a script in sight. It didn't have to dawn on me like a nightwalker that what they had in mind had nothing to do with the movie.

They pressed in on me from both sides. They were in their vampire costumes: black satin pants, jackets and shirts, black satin capes with blood-red linings. Their thighs and shoulders pushed into mine, their faces glowing and eyes shining in the candlelight. I was overcome with that same weird lethargy and wonderful languidity that I'd experienced back in Ted's office with them previously—the one I'd felt again watching their after-wrap performance with Ziggy the night before.

"We feel you need to understand our ... talents even better, firsthand," they both murmured, Boris gliding a pale hand up onto my beating chest, Karl gliding a pale hand down onto my bulging crotch.

Whatever *I* needed to feel, *they* could feel my heart throbbing in my chest and groin. And it excited them, and me—their hands touching, fingers playing. Time seemed to stand still, the air gone heavy, almost suffocating, my limbs grown weak and my heart and cock swelling strong. I couldn't move, couldn't get away if I desired. I had no purpose except that which they desired for me.

153

I was so suddenly and overwhelmingly entranced that I didn't even fully realize Karl was sucking on my hard cock until I looked down and saw my rigid appendage being consumed in his red, ravenous mouth. His dark head bobbed up and down in my lap, his soft lips sliding along my pulsating pink shaft, cool mouth squeezing and devouring me full-length.

Boris had my shirt open, his dark head bent down to my blond-fuzzed chest, his red tongue slapping at my stiffened pink nipples, swirling around them. He engulfed one with his lush lips and sucked on it as Karl sucked on my cock.

All foolish thoughts of escape drained out of me, my tissues surging with lust and my sinews melting with same. Only my cock and nipples stood tall, buzzing and shimmering, vacced and bathed by the wicked vampires, my balls bubbling with sperm.

Karl brought his head up. Boris dropped his head down. They switched mouth-positions on my chest and cock, Boris tonguing and suctioning my swollen prick now as Karl licked and sucked on my puffed-up nipples. My head bobbled with ethereal bliss and fell back onto the couch, stretching out my neck.

I was fully exposed to the pair of cock and bloodsuckers, wanting, needing, wallowing in the kiss and lick and suck and ... bite of the vampires. Boris nipped at the bloated hood of my cock. Karl nibbled at my blossomed nipples.

They could have attacked, finished me off without getting me off. And I would've welcomed it. But they had sexual needs of their own which, literally, came first.

I was stripped, lifted, lubed. Boris's cock sunk up into my anus, as I sunk down into his lap. I whimpered, my ass and cock swelling with roiling emotion. Karl straddled my spearing hard-on, stuck it into his ass, sat down on my pulsing erection facing me. It was a three-way man-stack: Boris fucking my ass from below, Karl anally riding my cock from above. His hand guided my hand to his rigid tool, and I grasped and stroked.

Their cool breath puffed into my face and against my neck as we began to move. Boris's cock churned back and forth in my chute as he pumped, Karl's anus gripping and sucking on my cock as he lifted up and down. My head lolled around and my eyes rolled back in my head, the rocking motions filling my cock-stoked anus and anus-sheathed cock with bodily bliss.

We seemed to move faster, with more force. I couldn't be certain. I was practically unconscious, riding the sexual high to the very pits of despair, if required. I was jerked up and down, the vampires moving in perfect unison, cock driving my ass driving my cock into ass. I was facing sweet unblessed oblivion, selling my bent soul for the best—and last—orgasm of my life. A fuck for the ages!

Boris growled in my ear, reaming my anus. Then he shuddered beneath me, shot cool cream into my burning chute. Karl growled in my other ear, bouncing on my cock. And then he shuddered, too, his cock jumping in my hand, shooting cool cream onto my heated chest.

I vaguely felt Boris's teeth pierce the right side of my neck, Karl's teeth the left. And then I shivered and spasmed and spurted and spurted and spurted and …

"Say, fellows! Take a looksee at what Heinie came up with for the film's climax!"

It was Ted, bursting into the trailer and shining a cross-shaped white light, from the baby spot he was holding, directly onto my forehead.

Boris and Karl hissed and yanked their fangs out of my neck, jerking their heads away from my holy spotlighted face. Just in time.

"Saaay! It looks like you boys got a little carried away with rehearsal!" Ted opined, gripping the spotlight and grinning.

God bless him!

155

Fangs for Francie, Bangs for Bobby, retitled *The Horror on Hillcrest Lane,* was a modest box office success by most movie mogul standards and a blockbuster smash hit by Ted Pine's C picture credos. Critics called it "raw, unnerving, low-budget realism at its best," and audiences swooned and swallowed in their seats. Boris Leturno and Karl Belgrade were universally hailed for their "chillingly effective" performances, the best since the monster mania days of the thirties and forties.

Ted had finally hit the big time, on the small horror scale. But at what price? His living soul, perhaps? The price of success in any Hollywood endeavor, probably.

I didn't stay around to find out, or share in the hoopla. Once filming wrapped up that night in Griffith Park, I was onboard the next eastbound freight headed for New York. I figured I'd try my hand at a nice, peaceful, sane line of authorial work—like writing insurance policies, maybe.

INHUMAN ECSTASY

P.A. Friday

It hurts at first, more than you could have imagined. Hot, deep, searing pain that even now makes your body jerk away, desperate for escape. But the burning fades more quickly each time. It dies away to a slow warmth which fills your limbs with lassitude. You can feel your blood trickling away, trace its path from your beating heart to his mouth pressed firmly against your neck. Your cock stirs under this assault of your senses—filling, growing; taking you up and up before you float away on a sea of pleasure. Nothing compares to this. It is beautiful and deadly, and not unlike Russian roulette. Each time it could be your last …

Mark was used to summing people up quickly, relying on a mixture of observation and instinct. His first glance at the guy sitting at the far side of the bar told him *gorgeous*. The second, stronger than the first, *dangerous*. The third, strongest of all: *I want him*. A bad idea? Oh, hell yes. Mark was no fool; his dark haired Adonis should be avoided at all costs. But Mark liked danger. Sometimes he thought he was addicted to it. He picked up his glass of ale and strolled across to sit next to the man.

"New around here?" he asked, with the obligatory blandness of small talk.

The man smiled, all lips and no teeth. "You could say that."

Mark indicated the guy's glass. "What are you drinking?"

A damn foolish question: The deep red spoke of wine or port. "Burgundy," the man said. He lifted an eyebrow. "Like to taste?"

In truth, Mark would rather not. But that was surely a come-on and he wasn't going to let it pass. "Don't mind if I do."

The stranger passed the glass, and Mark (remembering something he'd seen critics do on TV) sniffed it before raising the drink to his mouth. The smell was curious: less fruity than Mark had expected, though the pungency of alcohol was evident. He sipped it cautiously, and for a moment, he had the absurd feeling that he must have bitten his lip without realizing; the drink had the rusty iron spoon taste Mark associated with blood. But that sensation faded as sour, acidic alcohol spread across his mouth. He swallowed bravely, wondering why anyone would drink this stuff willingly. He took a large gulp of ale to clear his mouth of the taste, then offered it to the other guy.

"Fancy some ale?"

The man shook his head reluctantly. "Alas, I have an allergy."

Mark hadn't known anyone existed who actually used the word "alas." "I'm Mark," he said abruptly.

The stranger quirked his lips in what Mark presumed was as smile. "Alain."

They chatted lightly about various topics—the price of alcohol, the latest news stories. But Mark was aware at all times of another unspoken conversation taking place. Alain was checking him out. And Mark was sure as hell checking Alain out. He wanted to fuck Alain, and he wanted to do it tonight. Right now, preferably. So, when Alain's wine was nearly finished, he went on the attack.

"You know I want you." There was no reason to skirt around the facts. It was evident that Alain knew how he felt, and equally obvious that Alain was interested in return.

"Indeed. And you know I want you." Alain's expression was unreadable. "What you don't know is how."

Mark raised his eyebrows. Alain was a kinky bastard, then. It was hardly a shock. "Surprise me."

Alain looked him over, head to toe. His expression was quizzical. "No," he murmured finally. "Not tonight. Tonight is for you, Mark, to see if you can surprise *me*." His smile this time was almost predatory. "I should warn you, however, that I am not easily surprised."

Mark laughed at that. His would-be lover certainly didn't seem backward about coming forward: Mark had known that from the moment Alain held out his glass of burgundy. He thought about his bedroom, which took up the entire second floor of his apartment.

"Come with me," he said.

The short walk home was a quiet one. Alain seemed polite but distant. Willing but reserved. The conversation was superficial, but Mark got the idea that Alain was saying more than the words that came from his mouth. He just wasn't sure what the man was trying to tell him.

Alain raised an eyebrow when they reached the door to Mark's apartment. And raised it higher still as Mark led him upstairs to the bedroom. The room itself was warm, a pleasurable temperature to be naked in. The bed was large, with solid wooden bedposts and crisp clean sheets which Mark was looking forward to disheveling. He always kept the room immaculate, so that any visitor could enjoy himself in comfort.

"A civilized room," Alain commented. "An even better bed."

"Oh, I have no intention of being 'nice' in bed," Mark replied. "Come here."

They hadn't even done so much as kiss yet. Something about this affair was back to front and peculiar. It was as if Mark had ended up on a roller-coaster when he thought he was getting in a sensible saloon car. Alain stepped towards him, and Mark noticed that they were the same height, almost to the inch. One or other of them needed only to lean in a little way, and they would be …

(They were.)

… kissing. Alain had a certain reserve: He wasn't a thrusting tongue-and-teeth kisser. It was as if he were holding something back. But yet he was a willing visitor to Mark's apartment, and his hands were exploring Mark's body with a great deal of interest and skill. One of them moved up underneath Mark's shirt to touch his nipple with a fingernail while the other slid down, grabbing Mark's ass and pulling him closer so that they were groin-to-groin, two hard cocks pushing against each other through the fabric of their trousers.

Naked bodies touching, Alain's pale white skin a contrast to Mark's more tanned body. Sweat and heat and desire, yet still this curious sense of reserve in Alain, so that however much Mark asked of him, he didn't feel he was getting Alain's all. Why he should feel this way, Mark couldn't tell. Alain matched him stroke for stroke—he certainly wasn't a shy lover, but there was something missing.

Mark on his knees, his mouth around Alain's cock, sucking in the whole length before leaning back to start again. Alain's breath whispering out in small gasps, rocking back and forth to encourage Mark to continue, to suck there, to lick here, to go deep down until Mark's head was almost flat against Alain's belly. And Alain was so willing—yet not wholly taken up with Mark. Part of his mind seemed to be elsewhere.

Mark redoubled his efforts, determined to make Alain break apart for him. He pushed Alain onto the bed, his mouth slipping further back to lick at Alain's hole, breaching him first with tongue before using lubed up fingers. But even then … even as Mark slipped the condom on, even as he entered Alain—even as he brought Alain to his peak, and they both fell into orgasm, almost simultaneously … Alain was present but not-present.

They fucked again after that. Alain was appreciative, and his stamina was impressive. And in turn, he was willing to touch in many ways—though his kisses remained almost chaste in comparison. They fucked until the early hours of the morning, until Alain finally rose and dressed.

As Mark saw him to the door, Alain's eyes were dark and unfathomable. A final, quick kiss, before he said calmly, "Thank you for an enjoyable evening."

The phrase rubbed Mark the wrong way—it sounded like a brush-off. "You're welcome," he said, his voice slightly cool.

"I have offended you." Alain put a hand on Mark's shoulder. "Sometimes I do not express myself in the way I intend. I got great pleasure from this evening, believe me. You are an unusually talented man." His dark eyes flicked over Mark, as if assessing him. "I would like to return the compliment. If you would like to visit me tomorrow evening—tonight, I suppose I should say—I will make you most welcome."

"Thanks." Not a brush-off, then. Mark was disconcerted, but determined not to show it. He was damned if he'd let Alain just walk all over him. He was going to make the man feel something, whether he liked it or not. "I'd like that."

Alain's lips curled in that now-familiar closed-mouth smile. "My address is 304 Grace Street," he said softly. "Shall we say nine p.m.? I can show you a few things of my own."

Grace Street. Mark was impressed. Alain must be pretty much a millionaire. He wondered whether that was where Alain's sense of reserve came from—a suspicion that men must be after his money rather than him.

"Nine p.m. Grace Street," he said. "I'll see you then."

Mark dressed carefully the following evening. Nothing too posh, nothing to make him look as if he was trying too hard. A dark blue shirt. Smart trousers. His polished Italian shoes. Looking in the mirror, he thought that he scrubbed up pretty well when he tried. He'd bought a bottle of wine that afternoon, going by the wine seller's recommendation as his own knowledge was nonexistent. As he had done with the clothes, he'd gone for a middle price range: nothing too extravagant, but not a "two-for-a-tenner" bargain.

It felt curious strolling down Grace Street with the intention of entering one of the buildings. Mark did his best to look unconcerned, as if he belonged here, and to his surprise it worked—a couple of people nodded in passing to him, clearly taking him for a resident. By the time he rang Alain's doorbell, he was feeling quite confident.

"Hello?" Alain's voice.

"It's Mark."

At the sound of the buzzer, Mark pushed open the door and took the elevator to the third floor. The surroundings were sumptuous. When he got to Alain's door, it was already open, and Alain was standing there, resplendent all in black.

"Welcome to my home," Alain said.

"Nice," Mark said, trying to sound offhand about it.

"I have organized it to my liking. It took quite some time to get it so."

Mark grinned. Alain was forty at best, but sometimes he spoke as if he were an elderly gentleman.

"Looking good."

And this time Mark didn't just mean the apartment. He'd known

162

Alain was drop-dead gorgeous, but he looked incredible tonight. Mark could have ripped Alain's clothes from his body and taken him right there in the entrance hall. He took a deep breath, trying to cool his ardor a little.

"Tonight it is my turn, I believe, to show you what I can offer," Alain said, shutting the door behind Mark and ushering him into the lounge.

His voice seemed strange—strained, as if holding on hard to his self-control. It was peculiar: Last night, Alain had been an active and willing participant, but had never seemed in danger of losing his air of cool enjoyment. Tonight, however, he was almost quivering with arousal. Mark could see already the telltale bulge in Alain's black trousers. Whatever it was that Alain intended to show him tonight, it clearly turned him on like nothing else.

"You seem keen," Mark said lightly, trying to break the tension he could feel like static in the air.

Alain's eyes were as near to black as they could be. Mark was reminded once again of his early instinct: This man was dangerous.

"I like you," Alain said slowly.

"Good." Mark tried a grin in another attempt to lower the intensity, but Alain shook his head.

"I give you a choice …" He smiled, showing his teeth, and for a moment it was as if the universe had stopped for a few seconds. It was the first time Mark had noticed Alain's teeth … Alain's *fangs,* his confused mind corrected him. Common sense told Mark that he couldn't be seeing what he seemed to be seeing: It must be some fancy-pants dentistry that Alain had paid for. Yet instinct told him that his eyes were not deceiving him—the fangs were real. The surge of adrenaline and the uncomfortable thumping of his heart could have been fear or arousal—fuck or flight. Even Mark was not sure which it was. He met Alain's eyes.

"Yes," said Alain, giving the word a sibilant hiss on the final letter, "I am precisely what you are telling yourself I cannot be. And I give you three choices. The first"—he smiled cynically—"the most sensible option: run. Run away, little human fool. Be safe, be sensible, be gone."

Mark took one step backwards, towards the door of Alain's apartment. "And the others?"

"The first choice is the best one."

Was Mark being encouraged to leave or challenged to stay? He stood his ground—he was closer to the exit than Alain was—and waited for Alain to continue.

"Option two: You *think* you've experienced orgasm. You have 'died the little death' so many times. But this ... this could make those others seem insignificant, a mere echo of the real thing."

"The catch?" asked Mark, knowing that there was one.

"It will not only be the little death which you die." Alain reached out just one finger, running it down the side of Mark's face. "I will lull you, lust you, satisfy you—and kill you. I will do this not by choice—but the route to that particular ecstasy is a one-way trip. No returns. A death, yes—but a death more glorious than any other. You will rejoice in your passing, welcome it with ineffable joy. I can give you something humans can't even dream about, but the price is your life."

What shocked Mark was how much he wanted to say yes. Alain's voice was almost hypnotic, and Mark's desire surged through to the surface, his aching cock dying for the vampire's touch. *Literally* dying for it, Mark reminded himself.

"And the third offer?" His voice did not sound like his own: It creaked and grated like a gate in need of oiling. He felt as if he had drunk alcohol stronger than any he'd previously experienced. Real life seemed fuzzy and indistinct.

"The way of pain." Alain's voice seemed deeper, darker. "Pleasure, yes—but you pay for your pleasure with pain more searing than you have ever known. If you wish to live, I cannot anaesthetize you in the way I could to pave your path to death. You will feel pain, every hot, stabbing, throbbing beat of it. Every agony there is. You will, perhaps, wish or even beg for death but I will not be able to give you what you desire."

Run, you idiot. Run.

"Why …" Mark coughed, trying to rid himself of the chocking obstruction to his airways, which was fear itself. "Why would anyone choose that?"

"Why indeed?" agreed his vampire lover. "Because it, too, brings ecstasy. You will walk in the valley of death but you will not cross over to walk with Death himself. I will bring you back, inch by wild, joyful inch. You may feel dizzy and confused for a few hours, but you will recover." He looked pensive. "Very few mortals reach Death's valley and survive."

Mark felt his stomach turn over. He had known this man—this whatever-he-was—was trouble from the moment he saw him. What had possessed him to walk headfirst into this? But it was too late for self-recrimination now. Instead, he raised his chin, put on his battle armor of humor, and said, "So 'die,' 'want to die,' or 'run away'? You drive a pretty poor bargain, Alain."

The vampire was drawn into a surprised laugh. "I knew I liked you," he said.

"I'm flattered."

Alain gave a rueful little smile. "Shall I show you out?"

Mark should have said yes. He should have said yes right then. "No."

"No?"

"I must be mad," Mark mumbled to himself under his breath.

"Quite possibly," Alain agreed, startling Mark. Alain's hearing was more acute than he'd realized. "If you are not leaving, however, the question is: Which do you choose? In your words: 'die' or 'want to die'?"

Mark leaned against the edge of the sofa. "I'm quite attached to being alive, as a matter of fact. You make death seem extremely appealing, but I don't think I'm ready for that yet."

"It will hurt," Alain warned again. "More than you can imagine."

Mark took a deep breath. "Time to test my imagination, then," he said.

Alain led him into the bedroom. Where Mark had a wooden bed frame with crisp white sheets, Alain's bed was glass and metal, silk purple sheets lying sensuously across it. And God, Mark wanted to be in that bed with Alain, fucking. Whereas instead—

It was almost impossible for human teeth to pierce the skin, Mark knew. He had tried once—the result of a foolish bet when he'd been fifteen years old. The attempt had left deep red indentations in his arm for several hours. When these went, they were followed by an oval bruise, each tooth mark clearly identifiable, which had faded from blue to yellow over time. His mother had fussed and scolded when she saw it. He wondered what she would say now.

He felt Alain's eyes on him, and he turned to look at the vampire. Alain looked serious. "You are sure?" he asked. "I will not ask again."

Mark was sure and unsure in equal amounts. The one thing he did know was that if he walked away now, he would always wonder—always regret. He ignored the question.

"Dressed or undressed?" he countered.

"Undress for me, Mark." There was a longing look in Alain's face. Mark wasn't sure whether it was lust or hunger. Prey or partner? He would find out soon enough. He stripped off his top, his eyes on Alain. Then his hands sank to his fly.

"Do it," hissed his lover.

Mark smiled. Live for the moment? It felt—almost—worth dying for, to see that expression, that look of outright need, on Alain's face. Alain took a step closer, and Mark unzipped his trousers. Slowly, motion by motion, he began to drag them over slim hips and muscular thighs. When they got to his ankles, he slipped his socks off, too, until he was standing, naked, just by Alain's bed, his cock throbbing and hardening. Alain had been a more than willing partner last night, but tonight ... Mark's gaze dropped once more to Alain's tight trousers, which were doing nothing to conceal the vampire's arousal.

"Lie on the bed for me, Mark." Alain's voice was seductive and warm. Mark was mesmerized, almost mindlessly willing to do Alain's bidding.

One of Alain's hands slid down to cup the obvious erection at his own groin. "Aren't you a little overdressed for the occasion?" Mark asked softly.

It was only a flicker of time before Alain was nude. Mark's eyes lingered on that throbbing, purple-red cock which pushed up towards Alain's porcelain-white belly. Mark swallowed down the worst of his desire for Alain to penetrate him, to fuck him hard into the silken sheets.

"Ready?" Alain asked, sliding onto the bed.

Mark nodded, and Alain lowered his head to Mark's neck, lips open to bare sharp white fangs, which pierced his skin ...

Mark screamed. The noise seemed to reverberate around the large bedroom, sound bouncing off every wall, and each wall curving in to kill him. Oh God, he hadn't imagined—couldn't possibly have imagined—this level of pain. It was so intense that Mark couldn't even try to pull away: his entire self seemed focused on surviving. Or dying? Alain had promised not to kill him, but Mark was alone in a bedroom with a predatory vampire. How the fuck could he possibly trust anything Alain said?

But none of it mattered. Mark's consciousness was taken up by the tornado currently tearing his body to bits. He was no longer whole, merely a collection of atoms being split and split and split again, cruelly, remorselessly. How long had he been lying across the bed, Alain's fangs draining blood from him? Time was a nonsense, a pulling and stretching of reality. Days could have passed. All he knew was that he could not bear a moment more.

But the agony was definitely decreasing. Mark could begin to think again, be more aware of his body rather than feeling like a twisted ball of pain. And to realize that, against all odds, Alain had been telling the truth. Light-headed from the loss of blood, Mark was still aware of other parts of his body. Almost inconceivably, his cock was stirring, stiffening and growing by the second. It was …

("Yes, God, please, Alain …" Mark's words were desperate, almost incoherent, as he begged for more.)

… sensual, insanely sensual. Erotic pleasure suffused the pain. Mark was molten desire in the shape of a man. He was still aware—indeed, hyper-aware—of Alain's mouth on his neck, sucking remorselessly, sucking away not just Mark's blood but his human frailties. Guilt, shame, anxiety, melancholy—they flowed out of Mark, leaving him almost cleansed. And Alain's fingers were trickling over his body, lighting little flames of need wherever they touched. Lingering at long last on Mark's erect cock. Slender fingers which were neither hot nor cold. Simply perfect, like Alain himself. Lassitude engulfed Mark: He needed (wanted) nothing more than to lie against the silken sheets, offering body, soul, *everything* up to his vampire lover.

Alain was sucking more gently now—almost suckling, as a babe might on its mother's breast. Warming, comforting, reassuring—but the comfort flowing from baby to mother, from Alain to Mark. The pressure was slowing. Mark could feel tapered fingers sliding all the way around his erection, holding him firmly as the mouth on

168

Mark's neck grew gentler. Until Alain was merely kissing the surface of Mark's skin before leaning back to look deeply into his eyes. Mark was warm all over, burning in places. Alain's mouth was stained with Mark's blood, and Mark should have found that odd, even unpleasant, but how could he when he had found this level of pleasure?

"You are all right?" the vampire whispered.

Mark's "mmm" became a groan of need as Alain slid down his body to put blood-stained lips around Mark's cock. And that was so good. Mark groaned and fell into the abyss of orgasm. Death, or the "little death." At that moment, he would not have cared which it was.

Slowly, slowly, Mark drifted back to an awareness of where and who he was. The sensation of the sheets against his skin, smooth and cool. A faint pain in his neck where Alain's mouth had sucked his life blood from him. A male body beside him, smelling of sex and blood. And Mark himself, inexpressibly changed by his close brush with death. For he could have died: Mark knew that much. He had looked over the brink, and only Alain could have brought him back. It should be frightening. On one level, it still was—the last logical parts of Mark's brain told him how foolish, how dangerous this experience had been. The rest, though. The rest would visit hell itself to feel like this one more time.

"Alain?" he mumbled.

"Here."

Alain's voice was deeper, calmer, less dangerous than before. As Mark blinked bleary eyes to look at his lover, he could see that Alain, too, was sated—content like a well-fed cat.

"You meant it," Mark said.

Alain rolled over onto one side so that he was looking at Mark. "Which bit?"

Mark smiled. "All of it. You kept your promise."

"Did you doubt me?"

"I hardly know you."

"You do now."

Alain looked steadily into Mark's eyes, and Mark realized that the expressions which he had found so hard to read were now clear to him. He understood Alain in a way he'd never understood another person before. It wasn't love—one could love without understanding—but something stranger. Not romance, but knowledge. Not adoration, but a shared secret. They *knew* each other, on a soul level.

If vampires had souls.

"How?" asked Mark.

Alain stretched and shrugged. "How is the grass green? It just *is*." He leaned over and kissed Mark, and Mark could taste himself on Alain's lips.

"Am I a vampire now?"

Alain smiled. "No. Of all things in my creed, that is forbidden. But we are bonded, you and I." His eyes gleamed wickedly. "We share the same blood—yours."

"But this feeling, this—whatever it is… does it wear off?"

"Yes. In time."

"And then?"

"You are as you were," the vampire said quietly.

"Could we do it again?"

There was a pause.

"It is dangerous," said Alain. "It gets more dangerous every time. You lose a bit more of yourself."

"And then I die."

"Yes."

Somehow, Mark had not expected such a blunt answer, even though he should have known Alain now. And yet—was the chance of death an inhibitor or an encouragement?

"How many times?" he asked abruptly.

"I beg your pardon?"

"How many times before I die?"

Alain shrugged. "It depends." He hesitated before continuing. "That is why I have never tried before."

Mark sat up so he could see Alain more clearly. "I was your first?"

"Yes." Alain smiled. "You were my first."

It was Mark's time to be silent. "But you would do it again?" he asked at last.

Alain's eyes traveled over him, appreciation clearly visible. "With you?" he murmured. "Oh yes, I would do it again." He propped himself up on one elbow to kiss Mark, faint traces of blood still clinging to his mouth. "I should not, of course, but I would. If you asked."

"Someday," said Mark carefully, "someday. But not now—I will ask."

It hurts at first, more than you could have imagined. Hot, deep, searing pain that even now makes your body jerk away, desperate for escape. But the burning fades more quickly each time. It dies away to a slow warmth which fills your limbs with lassitude. You can feel your blood trickling away, trace its path from your beating heart to his mouth pressed firmly against your neck. Your cock stirs under this assault of your senses—filling, growing; taking you up and up before you float away on a sea of pleasure. Nothing compares to this. It is beautiful and deadly, and not unlike Russian roulette. Each time it could be your last …

SEXUAL TRANSITIONING

Ryan Field

The night Anton and Digger decided to turn Leo would haunt Anton throughout eternity. He hadn't wanted to turn him that soon. He'd wanted to think about it and talk it over with Leo to see if he was ready to become a vampire. Of course, Digger—always the bad boy careless one—shrugged and laughed it off. He'd wanted to turn Leo much earlier.

Anton hadn't expected to fall in love with Digger and Leo at the same time. Nor had he expected his feelings to be reciprocated by both. The concept of three so completely different men loving each other this way would at best be described as complicated under normal circumstances. But when two of the lovers were vampires it veered into pure unabashed confusion.

The night they turned Leo, they were on their way home from the nightclub. If that truck hadn't come from nowhere, or if Leo hadn't walked into the middle of the street without looking, there would have been time to talk and plan and organize the future in a more coherent way. Leo would have had time to adjust to the idea being a vampire and maybe his transition wouldn't have been so intense and violent.

There were nights after the accident, after they'd turned Leo, where Anton and Digger would talk about what had happened and shake their heads. Digger remembered it differently than Anton. Maybe he hadn't been paying attention, which Anton knew wouldn't have been unusual. Digger didn't even remember Leo in the middle of the street dying, his leg severed, losing so much blood he could barely speak. But Anton would never forget that night, not a single detail. If he closed his eyes, he could still see Leo look up at him and say, "I think I'm dying, Anton. Hold me. Don't let me go. I love you both so much." Nothing in Anton's mortal or immortal life had ever left such an impact on him.

After they turned Leo right there in the middle of the street, they brought him back to Digger's apartment in Newark. They figured he would be safe there. Anton had to deal with some family business the following night, but Digger could stay with Leo to make sure he didn't get into trouble. Newly turned vampires have different reactions. Some are calm and slide right into their new immortal lives without a hitch. Some can be moody and won't speak for days. Others can be nasty and all they want is to make the first fresh kill and suck human blood. Anton once saw a newly turned vampire crawl into a hole in the ground and refuse to come out for months. He drank the blood of voles and moles. In Leo's case, Anton didn't think there was much to be worried about because Leo had been such a sweet, tender, kind human.

But when Anton returned to Digger's apartment after dealing with his family business, and he found Digger naked and spent on the sofa and newly turned Leo stark naked staring at him with a glazed look. Anton felt a thump in his stomach and knew something had gone wrong. Instead of being moody or depressed, Leo was so high on becoming a vampire his feet hardly touched the floor. But more than that, instead of being hungry for blood like most newly turned vampires, Leo was hungrier for men, and for dick. He didn't even wait for Anton to set his car keys down or remove his jacket. He just went down on the floor, opened Anton's zipper, and started sucking Anton's cock.

At first, Anton didn't think it would be too much of an issue. Digger was a slim, sexy muscular vampire with the lanky body of a twenty-eight-year-old and the dick of a trashy-looking million dollar porn star. He had dark longer hair, constant stubble on his face, and a rough, dirty bad boy appeal that could turn heads wherever he went. It was the unwashed look that made him so appealing to both men and women. Anton knew he could turn heads as well. With his lighter hair, football player look, thick cock, and more conservative preppy appeal, he figured between the two of them they could keep Leo sexually satisfied until he passed through the transition period. After that, Anton knew he wouldn't have to worry about anything.

They went through a week of nothing but taking turns fucking Leo to satisfy his needs and urges. They fucked him on his back, on all fours, sideways, and upside down. At some points during that week, Leo would be so aroused and his vampire powers so heightened they wound up fucking him in mid-air, circling Digger's living room, waiting for Leo to cum. It wasn't that they minded. Both Anton and Digger found Leo so attractive it was hard to keep their hands off him. And it wasn't just sex. They both loved him and wanted to spend eternity with him. Unlike them, Leo was smaller and had a narrower frame. His feet were smaller and his legs more shapely, almost crossing the line of femininity. The muscles Leo had were delicate and defined by less obvious lines and bulges than Anton's and Digger's. He didn't have their broad shoulders, but he had a tiny waist and an ass that jutted out at the small of his back and rounded into a perfect heart shape.

But by the end of that first week, Digger and Anton could barely climb out of their oversized coffin at dusk. They didn't even get a chance to open the lid some nights. Leo would slide between their legs and start sucking their dicks right in the coffin. They'd lost time at work and they'd had to make excuses as to why they needed time off.

When a week had passed and Leo showed no signs of slowing down, Digger sighed and turned to Anton. "I think he's going to suck my dick right off if this continues. I thought this was supposed to stop." He reached down to massage his flaccid cock, as if to make sure he still had one.

He looked exhausted. Anton felt so sorry for him that he reached over and started to massage Digger's dick himself. "Under normal conditions it does wear off," Anton said. Digger spread his hairy legs wider so Anton could massage his balls, too. "But evidently when two very strong vampires turn a human, the results can often be *un*usual. I think that's what happened with Leo. We're both very strong, and he's still in shock … in a transition period."

Digger spread his legs wider and said, "Fuck, man, don't stop playing with my nuts. It feels so good to just have you massage me and I don't have to actually do anything."

Anton leaned over and he kissed Digger's balls. "Poor baby," he said. "But I think I have an idea."

"What? I'll do anything," Digger said. "I never thought I'd say this, but I'm so sick of sex and ass …"

"I hear you, buddy," Anton said, as he sat back and continued squeezing Digger. "I think to get Leo back to normal we need to shock him. We have to figure out a way to shock him with too much sex."

Digger sent him a horrified glance. "More than what he's already getting? I don't think I'm strong enough for that, dude."

Anton laughed. "I overheard a couple of guys at the nightclub talking about this photo shoot," Anton said. "There's this British Rugby team and some US Football team that both do these nude calendars for charity every year. And it just so happens that both teams are going to be in New York next week filming what's being called the ultimate jock calendar. And I have a feeling that's just what Leo needs: more jocks than he ever dreamed about."

Digger sat up and gaped at Anton. "Are you suggesting what I think you're suggesting?"

Before Anton could reply, Leo jogged into the living room with a blood mustache and a full erection. He jumped in between them and grabbed both their dicks. "Who wants to *fuck* now? I need a man bad. I want you both to *fuck* me at the same time again like you did last night. I'll climb up on Digger's lap and sit on his *dick*. Anton, you get behind me and start fucking me the minute I get Digger inside."

Digger and Anton exchanged a glance, and then Digger said, "Do whatever you have to do ..."

Although Anton had to call in a few favors to find out the exact details of the sexy jock photo shoot with the British Rugby team and US football team, in his search for information he ran across an old acquaintance he'd once met during a visit to London. The guy's name was Justin Langtree and he was the "kept" lover of the owner of the public relations firm that represented the British team. When Anton mentioned to Justin that he wanted to throw a huge party at his nightclub in New Jersey for the guys participating in the photo shoot—and then he explained why—Justin, a vampire who'd been turned in the 1970s, found the concept amusing: "You want to throw a huge party for the guys so they can gangbang this newly turned vampire slut who's in transition and out of control with sex?"

"I'll pay for everything," Anton said. "Make it clear I'll provide limos and anything they need to get here. I'll supply all the booze and food they need. I'm planning to use the biggest private room in the club and there will be male and female strippers. And the guys can invite anyone they want …"

On the night of the party, the only way to keep Leo from jumping out of the car on the way to the club and chasing every man in sight was to grab the back of his head and force it between Anton's legs. At one point, when they stopped for a red light and saw a rough-looking man talking on a cell phone on the corner, Leo started to pull down his pants and spread his legs. The guy standing on the corner looked into the car and dropped his phone when he saw Leo there, half naked. Anton hit the gas and pulled away fast.

As they pulled up to the club with a loud screech and stopped short, Leo was sucking the remaining drops of cum from Anton's dick. When he finally lifted his head and wiped his lips, he sent Anton a glance and said, "I'm sorry. I just can't help myself. I wish I had some control."

Anton rubbed the back of Leo's head gently. "Don't worry. I think you'll be fine soon. We'll get through this. I promise." Then he grabbed Leo's hand, lifted it slowly, and kissed his palm.

For an instant, it seemed as if Leo had calmed down a little. That desperate look seemed to have left his eyes. But the moment they entered the back room and Leo took one look at all the athletes and their friends, he grabbed Anton's hand and squeezed it hard. Staring from one young jock to the other, he said, "Can you smell it, Anton?"

"Smell what?"

Leo licked his lips. "The smell of hot young *men*. The scent of *dick*. It's everywhere. The room is filled with it. It's a combination of jockstraps, muscles, spicy deodorant, and sweat socks—everything that makes men what they are. It's the most intoxicating scent in the universe next to blood. I don't think I can control myself."

Anton scanned the room. The after-photo-shoot party had already been a few hours along and Digger was dancing with a guy and two girls at one end of a small dance floor to the kind of loud music Anton had always hated about this century. Anton released Leo's hand and said, "Have fun, baby. I don't want you to control yourself. Do you know what to do?" He was talking about a form of hypnosis all vampires can perform where they get mortals to do anything they want by just looking at them the right way and planting thoughts in their heads.

"I know what to do," Leo said. "Can I go now?" He stared at a group of young men drinking beer. "I need *men*. I need *dick*." The eager expression and the hungry look in his eyes caused a chill to run up Anton's back.

Anton kissed him on the lips and said, "Go have fun." It didn't bother Anton in the least to send Leo into a crowd of young men. Although vampires believed in love and long-term relationships, even more than mortals because their relationships lasted for centuries in some cases, it wasn't unusual for vampires to take on multiple sex partners. They knew how to separate emotion from sex.

As Anton and Digger stood off to the side and watched, Leo performed his vampire hypnosis on every stud in the room. There had to be at least two hundred young men. And by the time Leo was finished hypnotizing them two hours later, every one of them was watching him on the stage as he began stripping down for them. The female strippers Anton had hired stood there with their hands on their hips glaring at the way Leo commanded everyone's attention. So Anton and Digger paid them well and told them to go home.

When Leo was naked, he got down on his knees, turned around, and backed up to the screaming young men. And when he wiggled his ass in their faces and they started reaching for it, he spread his legs wider and arched his back for them.

Instead of what could have been absolute mayhem, the young jocks seemed to follow a set pattern without actually being told. When the first young jock jumped onto the stage and pulled down his zipper, Leo went down on his back and the guy kneeled over Leo's head. While the guy pulled his dick out of his pants, another guy jumped up on the stage and crawled between Leo's naked legs. He spread them apart, lifted them up a little, and then pulled his own dick out of his pants. First, he poured some beer on his cock, and then he poured some on Leo's ass. As he mounted Leo and went deep, the others stroked their dicks and waited for their turn. A line formed on the stage and the two guys who had fucked Leo first went to his sides, grabbed his legs, and held them open so each guy waiting his turn could get in and out faster. Each fuck lasted about a minute or two and each guy came. Although Leo didn't have to worry about sexually transmitted diseases because he was a vampire, Anton had provided free condoms to everyone so the guys themselves wouldn't be exposed to anything.

In one hour, at least a hundred guys fucked Leo senseless, and yet he *still* couldn't get enough dick. Anton felt a low-grade pain in his stomach as he and Digger exchanged frowns.

"We better face facts," Digger said. "He might never come out of this."

Anton didn't reply. About an hour after that, he noticed a huge pile of used condoms about six feet away from where the jocks were still taking turns on Leo. After a ginger jock dismounted and loped away, a tall muscular guy from the British Rugby Team crawled between Leo's legs and removed his pants completely. When the other drunken guys saw him remove his shirt and the rest of his clothes, Digger kicked the chair Anton was sitting on and said, "Oh fuck, this is getting worse."

As Anton glanced over to see Leo's expression, his eyes widened and he pressed his palm to his stomach. Leo's eyes had glazed over and he'd asked two of the guys who had been watching him get fucked to grab his ankles and spread his legs wider so the tall rugby player could slide right in. The rugby player didn't look like the rest of the guys. There was something different about him. His thick, unruly, wavy brown hair fell to the nape of his neck with wild twists and turns. His thick, bushy beard covered most of his chiseled features, including his lips. Although his smooth upper body created a contrast, his long fuzzy legs compensated for the hair he lacked on his upper body. In many ways he reminded Anton of a caveman he'd once seen in a book—all he needed to complete the look was a loincloth.

But Leo's face suggested eagerness and anticipation the moment the caveman grabbed his nine-inch erection and put on a condom. Leo nodded at the two beefy football players holding his ankles so they would open his legs wider. When they did, the caveman pointed the head of his dick to Leo's hole and stuffed it so fast and hard that Leo's head jerked forward and his eyes bugged out as if he were having some kind of seizure.

Anton and Digger exchanged a quick glance when they saw Leo's lips move. They couldn't actually hear what he was saying but they could read his lips. He was mouthing the words, "Fuck me harder, you hot fucking dirty stud!" and saying things that raised Anton's eyebrows. The other guys, still clearly under the hypnotic spell Leo had cast over them, shouted crude things like, "Fuck the bitch! Give that whore what he needs!"

One red-headed football player jumped up on the stage and shoved his dick into Leo's mouth while the caveman fucked. Another rugby player jumped up and rubbed his balls all over Leo's face. The caveman bit his lip harder and slammed Leo's ass with such intensity that the bottom's entire body jerked and another football player had to hold his shoulders to keep him from falling off the stage.

Digger flung Anton a glance and said, "We're in fucking trouble, man. I'm starting to think we could line up every guy in Newark and it still wouldn't be enough to satisfy him."

Anton felt a pull in his stomach. He remembered how innocent and sweet Leo was before they'd turned him, and he longed to go back in time and do things differently. "I love him so much."

In a rare show of emotion, Digger reached out and put his arm around Anton. "I do, too. But we might have to lock him up if this continues. I don't see any other way."

In rare cases, vampires who had been turned without warning and couldn't make it through the transitional stage eventually found themselves locked in coffins for eternity. Anton didn't want to think about that. He couldn't deal with the thought of losing Leo forever. "Let's just get through this night," he said, rubbing Digger's thigh.

The caveman's hips moved faster; he pounded Leo's ass with more force. Anton watched with parted lips because he'd never seen a mortal man fuck with such aptitude. In Anton's experience, most mortal men tended to move too fast and only cared about their own climax. But this caveman-jock-rugby-player broke all the rules. And it seemed to be driving Leo into what could only be described as a proverbial mindless state of ecstasy.

The caveman wound up pounding Leo's ass for about forty-five minutes. By that time the other guys had formed a semi-circle around the pair to cheer them on. When the caveman went deep one final time, his head went back and his body went dead still. His face turned a bright shade of red when he came and his fuzzy legs shuddered a few times. Leo came, too, and without even touching his own dick. He had a football player dick in his mouth and two guys from the rugby team were squeezing his chest muscles, which seemed to make his climax more intense. Anton understood this because he was a vampire. Every nerve ending in a vampire's body becomes heightened and exaggerated during sex, especially during climax—especially the nipples. He remembered the first time he'd had sex after he'd been turned and all the physical sensations it had brought to him. Only he hadn't lost control the way Leo had.

Digger and Anton watched as the caveman pulled out and smacked Leo's ass hard. When the caveman stood up and a stocky football player with a slight beer gut kneeled down between Leo's legs, Digger rolled his eyes. "Didn't that dude fuck him already?"

Anton shrugged. "I'm not sure. I lost track a while ago. I think a couple of guys fucked him twice."

Before Digger could reply, something interesting happened. As the stocky football player reached down to shove his middle finger up Leo's ass, Leo pushed two dicks away from his face and looked up at the football player. He said something Anton couldn't hear. But a moment after that, Anton heard the other guys moaning and groaning. The caveman returned to Leo's side and reached down to help him stand up. As he stood, Leo pressed his palm against the caveman's broad chest and smiled. The caveman returned the smile and reached back to rub Leo's ass a few times.

"What's going on up there?" Digger asked.

Anton shrugged again and stood up. "Let's go find out."

As they crossed the room, the caveman walked away, leaving Leo alone on the stage. Anton, watching Leo glance at the pile of used condoms and shake his head, told all the guys to get dressed and pull up their zippers. Then Leo, who didn't see Anton and Digger coming toward him, turned and started looking for his own clothes.

By the time Anton and Digger reached him, he'd picked up his pants and the other guys had gone back to the bar area as if nothing unusual had happened. Anton grabbed Leo's arm and asked, "What's going on?"

Digger held his breath, waiting for an answer.

182

Leo smiled at Anton and said, "I'm tired now. I'd like to go home. I've had enough sex."

Digger's eyes bulged. He leaned forward and took Leo's other arm. "Seriously, man. You're done? No more dick?"

Leo glanced around at the jocks, and then at the pile of used condoms, and said, "I'm done. I just want to go home now and snuggle up between my two big strong men." He leaned forward to kiss them both. "I feel different now. I can't explain it. And I can't believe all those guys just fucked me. I know it happened. I remember everything—but I've never been that way, guys. I don't understand …"

Digger put his arm around Leo's shoulder while Anton reached for his waist. Anton said, "We'll explain everything later, baby. Just get dressed and we'll take you home. You didn't do anything wrong."

Leo glanced around the dark bar at all the jocks and their buddies. "What about these sweet men?" he asked, his voice sounding softer, more like when he'd been human.

Anton laughed. "They won't remember a thing that happened tonight, other than being here and having a good time. They'll be just fine. After you get dressed you'll have to release them from the hypnotic spell, though. Do you think you can do that alone?" He knew Leo had been able to hypnotize them all earlier, but he wasn't sure he could reverse it now that he'd returned to normal.

"I think I can," Leo said. "They're all such nice guys I wouldn't want anything to happen to them, especially the big sweet guy with the beard over there. He's special for some reason." He pointed to the caveman who had fucked him the hardest. The caveman had put on his clothes and was talking to a couple of guys who were poking him in the chest and laughing.

"Special," Digger said.

Anton understood what Leo meant. He caressed Leo's face and said, "He's the one who shocked you out of transition and brought you back to us. If he hadn't been so powerful I don't know what we would have done."

"I don't get it, man," Digger said. "I thought it was the gangbang that did it."

Anton smiled at how little Digger knew about being a vampire, even though they'd both been vampires for a long time. "It *was* the gangbang," he said. "But that guy with the beard was the final touch. I'll explain it later."

"I feel like a first class whore," Leo said.

"You *were* a first class whore," Digger said.

As Digger and Anton turned to leave the stage so Leo could get dressed and release the guys, Digger asked, "Are you sure this is the end?"

Anton put his arms around Digger and led him to the door. "I'm sure. We've gotten through the worst of it. Now we just have to teach him how to hunt and how to mainstream just like us. He's smart and I don't think we'll have any issues."

As Digger sighed a breath of relief, Anton sent Leo a quick backward glance. When their eyes met, Leo smiled and Anton winked. For the first time since Anton and Digger had turned him, Anton didn't feel that nagging, endless pain in his gut as if he done something he'd never be able to reverse. Though he would never be certain he'd done the right thing by turning Leo, at least he had hope now.

TWICE SHY

Pink Rushmore

Lean and slight of build, Jack's perfectly-sized muscles twitched with anticipation as he pulled off his shirt, nipples sharp as cut diamonds, his rock-hard cock straining against his jeans.

I walked closer, took his face in my hands and softly kissed him. He responded shyly at first, but grew bolder by the second, urgently parting my lips and tangling his tongue with my own, as if this was the moment his mouth had been waiting for all his life.

My cock responded urgently—always in such a hurry, that cock of mine. I pulled back a little. I wanted to kiss him some more, to continue probing and savoring his taste, but Jack had other plans. He pushed his body closer—I could feel his cock throbbing against mine—it was enough to drive a guy mad. Jack's hand was fumbling at my zipper, but I pushed him away, knelt down and kissed his desire, and moved my way up to his left nipple. Jack moaned, and then gasped when I bit it lightly.

"Harder," he whispered, "Please harder." I was just about to oblige him when the fucking phone rang.

"Mullens, you're on the board," Tony bellowed in that foghorn voice of his, plowing into my fantasy. I screwed my eyes shut, tried to will Tony away. The phone rang again, "Quit your fucking daydreaming and answer the goddamned phone, Mullens."

I sighed. Jack and my cock would have to wait. I shook it off, checked my boner into Heartbreak Hotel, and pushed the speaker button that would broadcast our conversation to the rest of the team. Tony hit the tracking button and I picked up the phone. "Hi. This is Michael."

"Hi, Michael." The voice said. He sounded young from what I could tell, but he didn't offer any more information, so I asked him his name.

He said it was Wheel. I knew that joke, had heard it a million times, and so I said, "Your last name wouldn't happen to be Ferris, would it?"

"Not very original, am I," he said sadly. Of course, they all sounded sad—it was the nature of the work—but this boy's gut-wrenching hopelessness was palpable. "So, Wheel, what's going on tonight?"

"Not much," he said. "Just hanging out in my room."

His room? Not his apartment or house, so maybe high school, or college? "Where do you go to school, Wheel?"

"I don't," he said.

"So, when you say room …" I asked.

"I rent a room. They call it a bachelor's apartment, but it's just a room."

Just the way he said it conjured up a Tennessee Williams play—a small dank room, dimly lit, a broken neon sign outside the window that buzzed and annoyed like a drunken fly; inside broken dreams scattered on the worn rug.

"You sound sad, Wheel," I said, and a couple of the guys in the room snickered. Wheel thought that was funny, too, because he said, "Do a lot of happy people call a suicide hotline?"

"You got me there." I said, with a little chuckle. I wasn't being flip;

186

experience had taught me not to be too serious, or pushy—just let them tell their story in their own time. "What's up, Wheel?"

The silence on the other end of the line was almost deafening, broken only by a barely audible sob. There it was. Desperation.

The team began to pay more attention. Tony began to stab an eraser into the desk, while Skinny Joe leaned forward with a hungry look in his eyes. I gave him one back that said, *Calm the fuck down. You're getting ahead of yourself.*

The sobs had quieted. We were left in a moment of eerie stillness. A cricket would have been nice about right then. "Wheel? You still there?"

There was nothing for a moment, then a soft, "I'm here."

We all let out a sigh of relief. I had to know more about this kid, about why he wanted to take his own life—if indeed that was what he wanted to do, so I stepped up the banter. Finally got him to talk.

At twenty-one, he moved to New York after graduating from BYU in Provo because ... there was a pause and an intake of breath and then he came to the stinky truth of the matter: "They're all gone. My parents, everything I know, everyone I love—all because ..." There was another intake of breath as he said the words "... I'm gay."

Then there was a distant knocking on the other side of the line, and I was heartened because that meant Wheel wouldn't be alone, that I had some time. Relieved, I looked up to give my co-workers the thumbs up. That's when I noticed Skinny Joe was gone. It took me three seconds too long to put two and two together before I began to scream into the phone "Wheel! Whatever you do, *don't* answer that door! Do you hear me? Wheel?"

The phone went dead.

Skinny Joe

Suicide by vampire had seemed like such a brilliant idea, but all that lot wanted to do was fucking talk. And Joe was fucking *hungry.* Why try to save them? They were supposed to be the Make-A-Wish-Foundation for those who wanted off this ball of dirt. It was a win-win for everyone.

His long sinewy legs picked up speed with every second, his short cropped black hair rippling with every step. Skinny Joe was not as old as Michael or Tony, but he was young enough when he died, and dead enough now that he had a good deal of speed—and if they didn't notice he was gone, he had at least five minutes to make the seven mile trek to the kid's hotel.

The place was three floors of flea-infested ramshackle with a neon sign out front that just said "Ho"—the "TEL" having long since blinked out. Joe thought it was appropriate considering the lot coming and going.

Knowing just where to go—his voice recognition and hearing was remarkable—Joe bounded up the stairs, veins pulsing, mouth watering, cock throbbing. He was prepared to show this kid a good time before helping him shuffle off this mortal coil. His cock really wanted to do the knocking, but Joe used his knuckles instead.

The door opened a crack, and a small voice said, "Come in."

That was all Joe needed. He pushed the door open wide and stepped inside.

I heard the scream just as I approached the place. I sniffed the air, and caught a smell, stopped dead in my tracks. No. That couldn't be. I followed my nose to the third floor and hoped I wasn't too late.

The door was open, which is basically an invitation, so I stepped inside. Skinny Joe was trussed up by his feet and dangling in front of the window like an oversized swag lamp. A telltale glint of silver sparkled when the blinking neon light hit the rope. Now I knew how and why, but the question was who.

A soft voice answered my query: "Michael, I was hoping you'd come."

I turned. If I had a beating heart it would have leapt out of my chest.

My sense of smell was not wrong, but there were so many questions swirling around in my head. "Jack," I said, wanting nothing more than to hold him until the sun came up.

Instead, I punched him in the gut.

He responded by socking me good on the chin. We wrestled to the grimy floor, our faces inches apart. He was strong, but let's face it: I'm a vampire, so I had the upper hand.

"After thirty years, you had to do *this?*" I asked, socking him in the shoulder. "You couldn't have just called?"

"Yeah, well, after thirty years I wasn't sure you'd *take* my call." He smacked me a good one in the kidneys.

"Hey! Hey!" Skinny Joe yelled, still dangling from the ceiling, "You two assholes just going to go all Brokeback on each other and leave me hanging here?"

Jack and I stopped, shared a look, and it was as if no time had passed at all. He kissed me full on the mouth, then turned to Joe. "Wouldn't dream of it," he said, and pulled a crossbow from underneath the cot.

"Aw. Fuck me," said Joe right before Jack pulled the trigger and shot a stake through his heart.

It would have been shocking had I not known that Jack's a vampire hunter, but I did, so what did I expect? Therapy?

There was a wail of sirens, and they were getting closer. Jack grabbed his crossbow and said, "We should go." I pulled him to me, put my arm around his waist, and just before he wrapped his arms around my neck, he yanked the slender silver rope from the ceiling and shoved it in his pocket. I gave him a look, and he said, "What? These things don't grow on trees …"

We stood on the window ledge together and jumped into the night.

I've been a vampire for over a thousand years. Plus I'm a huge *Superman* fan, so I've had plenty of time to perfect a romantic landing. And I nailed it—me first, with Jack in the crook of my arm until I could put his feet softly on the ground—just on the other side of the cop cars.

Jack started laughing, "Show off."

Yeah, OK, maybe I was showing off a bit, but on the other hand … Jack.

We walked away at a leisurely pace—the vampire and the vampire hunter—two men in the dark of the night, and I, for one, was thinking about what could possibly happen next.

Jack

They walked together in silence for a while, Jack trying to figure out what to say next, Michael—who knows what Michael was thinking. Jack had never met a vampire like him in his entire life.

He'd kept track of Michael all these years, followed his every move. He felt a small pang of regret for the charade about the Mormon kid, but he needed to be with him again. Plus he'd been able to kill one of the bad guys, so as far as he was concerned it was a win-win.

Jack had known about Michael from the time he was old enough

190

to understand what he was born to be. Like his father, and his father before him, and all the way back as far as the family could remember, they were vampire slayers, and Michael had always been the one that got away. Ten generations of vampire slayers could not be wrong about one vampire, and Jack had grown up wanting to be the one that destroyed this creature.

Each generation had been unable to slay the beast. According to the stories passed down, at the last moment of battle, Michael had always smiled, his dark red lips curled above his fanged teeth, his azure blue eyes bright and sparkling as he leaned down and whispered the same words, "Not yet." And then he'd disappear into the blood-scorched night.

Jack's own first encounter with Michael had been, as memorable goes, on a scale of World War II. There'd been a clan of vampires feeding on goth kids attempting arcane rituals out of some necronomicon they'd found in an old bookstore. The fight had been brutal. He'd gotten there a few minutes later than he'd planned and had just started loading his crossbow when Michael appeared out of nowhere and, to Jack's surprise, he started slaying vamps right next to him. Jack was a stunned—vamps don't kill other vamps, yet this guy was clearly a vamp, and he was clearly killing other vamps. He'd actually introduced himself, said "Hi. Name's Michael. I take it you're the latest Van Helsing?"

And after it was over, and the kids had run away and there were five or so piles of dead vampire dust on the ground, their eyes met. Jack realized that this was *the vampire,* the one his family had vowed to take down. And God help him, all he wanted to do was kiss him. *What the fuck?* There was something so strong, so unmistakable between them, such chemistry that Jack was surprised the air hadn't exploded. The way Michael looked at him, the way his eyes smoldered with passion, like he already knew him. And how it came to be that they'd ended up spending one incredible moment—one indescribable moment in a time warp—he couldn't begin to tell you. But he knew he'd never be the same.

That night, Michael had sucked his cock to a size he'd never before achieved and then guided him up to his ass cheeks and into that glorious asshole. So tight, so cool—skin so soft it was its own lubricant. How at Michael's insistence he'd pounded and pounded, his flesh slapping against Michael's ass as Michael urged him on, "Deeper, harder, more!" until cum exploded from his cock in urgent spurts as Michael's ass muscles coaxed orgasm after orgasm from his body.

Afterwards when he held Michael, when he kissed him and was kissed so deeply and passionately in return, he knew what love was, he knew what lust was. Even though Michael's lips were close to his ear, Jack had just managed to make out the barely audible words, "I have waited so many lifetimes for you." And that was when Jack began to sob. He sobbed so hard he thought he would break. What the fuck was he doing? He knew this was wrong, yet every nerve in his body felt alive in a way he'd never before experienced.

The irony that fucking a dead man made him feel alive did *not* escape him.

And so, he'd given Michael up. Walked away and didn't look back. For thirty years, he only looked back one or two times a week. Maybe four if he was being honest.

And now, here they were again. Jack had orchestrated the whole thing, through lies, through manipulation, Jesus—how could he live with himself? He was about to tell Michael that this was a mistake when Michael reached down, took Jack's hand and entwined his fingers with his own. He turned ever so slightly, eyes a passionate question: "So, what next?"

Sweet Mother Mary of God, could he do it? Jack closed his eyes, squeezed Michael's hand, and smiled deep into those cool blue eyes. "You live around here?"

Being a vampire has its advantages. Being able to leap out of tall buildings in a single bound is one, and speed is another. There's a long list of bonuses, but they all pale in comparison to one thing: being alive. Really, truly loving a mortal is the only thing that comes close to breathing, to having a beating heart. And I hadn't felt alive since Jack left me thirty years ago. Not a word, not a note, not a sigh. I didn't try to find him because I'm a vampire and I'm not stupid. Loving me tore at his very core. And he made the honorable choice. Respect.

But now I didn't know what to think now. Hell, I *couldn't* think— all the blood in me was holding a party in my dick. Which is why I used my super speedy powers to get Jack back to my place and in my bedroom.

I undressed him, taking my time with each button, slowly revealing each smooth, ripple of muscle, the soft downy hair on his stomach that curled down and downward to the patch of light blond pubic hair nestled around his perfect, eager cock. I reached between his legs and ran my finger from his balls to his ass and slipped a finger inside. Jack shivered and then pulled me closer as I buried my face in his chest and clutched his ass cheeks, one in each hand.

Inch by inch I worked my way back up to his lips. I could have cum right then and there but his carotid was pulsing at a very rapid pace and, you know, as a vampire, that's a little hard to overlook. We needed to take it slower, much slower—but my cock tugged and strained at my pants so hard it was about to blow out the zipper.

Jack pulled my cock out of my pants, took his tongue and licked it from the tip to the bottom like a rocket pop. It was all I could do not to explode, as his lips slid up and down my shaft. I shivered as his tongue expertly swirled up, down, and around every inch of my throbbing pole. I began to feel heady and knew that if I didn't control myself that in a moment my fangs were gonna be growers. Out of fucking nowhere this commercial appears in my head and it's, *"How many licks does it take to get to the center of a Tootsie Pop?"* I burst out laughing because—come on, I'm over a thousand years old, and that's the fucking image I came up with to stop me from blowing my wad, and, you know … possibly killing my lover?

But it worked—my fangs went back in. Jack saw this, and I swear he looked a little angry.

"You OK?"

"Yeah, yeah. I just had—nothing. Sorry," he replied. He sat down at the foot of the bed, where his clothes were puddled on the floor, grabbed my hand and pulled me down to him and kissed me sweetly on the lips.

And then I'm not sure what the hell happened. I could feel something wrap around me, and then quite suddenly I was as weak as a kitten. Jack used the opportunity to push me back on the bed, and that's when I realized he was wrapping me in the silver rope. I was completely paralyzed, unable to move a muscle, although I did note that my cock was still rather merry.

Jack leaned forward then and whispered softly in my ear, his voice catching. "I'm sorry, I can no longer live this way."

Ooooooooh, I thought. *Now I get it.*

The older you get, the more you come to accept opportunities that you've missed. After a thousand or so years, I've had plenty of those. But mortal men, they have a smaller window of regret. Back in old times, people didn't live as long, giving them less chance for regrets. But this century was different, and Jack was torn between two worlds. The Van Helsing legacy—or the love of a vampire.

I was impressed that he loved me enough to actually kill me. I was actually touched.

"Don't be sad," I said, "Te in aeternum amabo." *I will love you forever.* (Hey—I'm old, I use the Latin sometimes.)

Then he did something kinda unexpected—he took my still-throbbing shaft in his hand and, before he slid his lips down over it, he said, "You are mine."

I groaned, and if I could have moved I would have arched my back as his mouth slid down further, completely engulfing my cock, his saliva and tongue exactly as I remember it. I wanted him to suck me off until I exploded inside his mouth—now *that's* a great way to die.

My cock was now gigantic, and even in my diminished state with the silver rope across my upper torso, those fangs were growers, bringing me thoughts of forever, thoughts of eternity. And that was when Jack took a knife from who the fuck knows where and slashed his wrist open in one fluid motion, his blood spilling on my chest, my face, and splashing across what I'd like to think was my soul.

I turned my head away, only to see his cock staring at me with its one good eye. I tried not to taste his blood, but it splashed into my mouth. And I tried not to drink, but *fuck,* man—I'm a goddamned vampire, not a vegan.

Jack hadn't expected Michael to have the strength to do anything besides drink, much less push him away, yet he flew back on the bed, hard. All of him. Some of the hard parts wanted to just fuck Michael until come-what-may, but he had started this, and he was going to finish it.

Jack pushed his arm and the gaping wound into Michael's mouth until nature won over nurture and Michael's his teeth clenched onto Jack's arm like a hungry kitten on a nipple.

Jack felt the euphoria of the blood leaving his body, his mind retreating to the past, that night of passion, of firsts, of forevers, of nevers—but before he could fully go there, a hand clenched over the spurting artery, and Jack opened his eyes.

Michael was staring at him. *Shit. He knew.*

What the fuck was happening here? I'd been tricked—totally blindsided. Hadn't seen it coming. I focused everything I had and struggled against the silver rope. The blood was flowing from Jack's wound, leaving him in no condition to stop me. With near Herculean strength and willpower I managed to shake the silver rope off most of my torso and grabbed his wrist and squeezed to stop the blood flow. I had a few fucking questions.

"Jesus, Jack," I said, "why didn't you just tell me?"

He smiled faintly, "I wasn't sure you'd approve."

"So, we couldn't just have a discussion about it …?"

"I'm dying, and you want to talk," he said, smiling weakly.

The thing is, he *was* dying. Before he'd called the hotline, before I'd kissed him, before he'd slashed his wrist. He was a very soon to be dead man. I'd tasted his disease.

"Only two things in my life have meant anything to me: One was my family's honor, the other was you. I'm not planning on giving up this life without one or the other. So, I thought I'd let you decide."

Well, that was one hell of a fucked up offer: feed on the man I have waited for all of my lifetimes and end his life—or feed on him and turn him into the thing he hated most, or I could die at his hand. What was a bloodsucker to do?

He smiled up at me weakly and I sighed, "You couldn't have waited until after I fucked you to slice your wrist open?"

He laughed a little. "I wasn't sure I could do it after."

"Coward." I thought for a moment, then made a decision. I grabbed the knife, opened my own vein and pushed his mouth to my wrist. "Drink," I said. "Drink and gain back some strength." He struggled against me, but even the tiniest bit of my blood give him strength, and I forced him to swallow it.

I could see the color coming back into his face and limbs, his body so happy that he couldn't help but drink. I watched his pink tongue lap up the blood oozing from my vein. "Drink," I said, stroking his cock as it, too, sprung back to life. "Then I'm going to fuck you so hard you're going to think you've died and gone to heaven. After that we can talk about a little something called eternity."

I had another look at his cock, which appeared eager to continue the conversation, then rolled him over and shoved my own demented soldier up in his ass as hard as I could. And I fucked that ass until neither one of us could take the friction or the heat any longer. In and out, skin slapping skin, flesh tearing flesh, pleasure mounting in both us until we shot our loads from here to fucking kingdom come. At that precise moment I dug my fangs deep into the side of his neck and drank. I drank until he was almost as white as I am, and then I asked him one final question: "Nunc te mihi in sempiternum?"

He smiled and answered weakly, "Yes, I will love you forever."

It was all I needed.

I positioned myself on top of him, buried his still-hard cock inside my own eager ass, and gasped at the perfection of the fit. But I couldn't think about that so much—I had to concentrate. I bit into his neck once again, and rode him up and down as I sucked the last bit of blood from his body. Despite the intensity of the situation, we both came again, in seemingly perfect unison.

Our bodies were spent, his pretty much lifeless. I collapsed on top of him, caressing that perfect body and kissing his dead, cold lips— ignoring the tears streaming down my face. I could still feel his heart beating weakly in his chest, and I held him until there was no beat, no breath, just a final sigh.

After a few minutes, I got up. I dressed quickly, then went to the window and jumped into the night.

Now, you may think this is a sad ending to my love story, but as I said before, the closest thing a vampire can get to feeling alive is to love a human. Yes, I could have turned him, that was an option—but if I had, neither of us would ever have the opportunity feel alive again. And that, my friend, would have been a true tragedy.

About the Editor and Authors

Born and raised in Normal, Illinois, **WINSTON GIESEKE** began writing short stories and plays at a young age to escape the banality of a healthy Midwestern upbringing. He relocated to Los Angeles at eighteen and received a degree in Screenwriting from California State University, Northridge, three years later. Kickstarting his career as a television writer, he penned episodes for shows like *Wildfire* and *Hollywood Off-Ramp* as well as the made-for-cable movie *Romantic Comedy 101*, which starred Tom Arnold and Joey Lawrence. While living in Los Angeles, he composed tantalizing copy for various adult entertainment companies (including Penthouse.com and Napali Video, home of "big boobs and catfights") and served as editor in chief of both *Men* and *Freshmen* magazines before honing his journalistic skills as managing editor of *The Advocate*. An award-seeking vocalist whose "rich voice harkens back to vintage Hollywood crooners" (Gay.net), his "saucy yet heartfelt" debut album, *On the Edge*, which "takes classic material, turns it upside down, and then spits it out with panache" (*Frontiers*), was released in 2012. He now resides in Berlin, an experience he shamelessly exploits at ExpatsInBerlin.us, and is the editor of the anthologies *Indecent Exposures*, *Daddy Knows Best*, *Team Players*, *Straight No More*, *Blowing Off Class*, and *Whipping Boys*.

DAVID APRYS hails from the Midwest but has also lived in Southern California, London, and the Deep South. He now makes his home in the Chesapeake Bay area. An unrepentant hedonist and keen observer of people, he's worked as an investigator, freelance magazine writer, and actor. He is currently hard at work on his first novel.

The author of several books—including the private eye novel *All White Girls*—**MICHAEL BRACKEN** is better known as the author of almost 1,000 short stories, including erotic fiction published in *Best Gay Erotica 2013*, *Flesh & Blood: Guilty as Sin*, *Freshmen*, *Hot Blood: Strange Bedfellows*, *Men*, *Model Men*, *Sexy Sailors*, *The Mammoth Book of Best New Erotica 4*, *The Mammoth Book of Erotic Confessions*, *Ultimate Gay Erotica 2006*, and many others. He lives and writes in Texas.

LANDON DIXON's writing credits include stories in the magazines *Men*, *Freshmen*, *[2]*, *Mandate*, *Torso*, and *Honcho*; stories in the anthologies *Straight? Volume 2*, *Friction 7*, *Unzipped*, *Wild Boys*, *Bad Boys*, *Black Dungeon Masters*, *Boys in Bed*, *Sex on the Mat*, *Lust in Time*, *Pay For Play*, *The Spy Who Laid Me*, *Latin Lovers*, *Indecent Exposures*, *Daddy Knows Best*, *Straight No More*, *Team Players*, *Ultimate Gay Erotica 2005/2007/2008*, and *Best Gay Erotica 2009/2014*; and the short story collections *Hot Tales of Gay Lust 1*, *2*, and *3*.

RYAN FIELD is the author of over 100 published works of LGBT fiction, the best-selling *Virgin Billionaire* series, a PG-rated hetero romance that was featured on the Home Shopping Network titled *Loving Daylight*, and a few more works of full length fiction with a pen name. He's worked in publishing for twenty years as a writer, editor, and associate editor. His work has been in Lambda Award-winning anthologies and he's self-published a few novels with Ryan Field Press.

Known mostly for her erotic fiction, which has come out with publishers worldwide, **P.A. FRIDAY** also writes regularly about disability and about the Regency Period (both often seep into her erotica), and has been known to branch out and write about almost anything! She hates coffee, drinks too much red wine, has an unnervingly large collection of *Doctor Who* DVDs, and blogs at PenelopeFriday. LiveJournal.com.

VINCENT LAMBERT, a New York-based journalist, blogger, and photographer, has covered the adult entertainment industry since 1996. He has written for numerous magazines, including *Adult Video News, GAYVN, XBIZ, Unzipped, Freshmen, Men,* and *Manshots.* Lambert also served as a judge for the GAYVN Awards for twelve years. His eponymous site, VincentLambert.com, features gay porn gossip and news. His short stories have been published in anthologies such as *Straight No More* and *Blowing Off Class.* Lambert is currently lead blogger for GayDemon.com.

BRETT LOCKHARD is a writer who lives in New York City with a bunch of succulents.

CHIP MASTERSON writes pornographic adventure fiction for people with muscle or strength fetishes, in a wide variety of styles and themes. There is little in the way of traditional "sex." Sometimes there isn't any at all. Much of this oeuvre may be freely viewed, with appropriate caution, in the adult section of Yahoo! Groups under the group "chipstories." His life is dominated by too many rescue animals in a rough but friendly section of Los Angeles, California.

GREGORY L. NORRIS lives and writes in the outer limits of New Hampshire. He once worked as a screenwriter on two episodes of Paramount's *Star Trek: Voyager* and is the author of the handbook to all things Sunnydale, *The Q Guide to Buffy the Vampire Slayer*. Norris writes regularly for various national magazines and fiction anthologies, and is a judge on 2012's Lambda Awards. Visit him online at www.gregorylnorris.blogspot.com.

ROB ROSEN (www.therobrosen.com), award-winning author of the novels *Sparkle: The Queerest Book You'll Ever Love, Divas Las Vegas, Hot Lava, Southern Fried, Queerwolf,* and *Vamp,* and editor of the anthologies *Lust in Time* and *Men of the Manor*, has had short stories featured in more than 180 anthologies.

NATTY SOLTESZ's novel *Backwoods* was a 2012 Lambda Literary Award finalist and features illustrations by Michael Kirwan. His stories have been published in magazines like *Freshmen* and *Mandate* and in anthologies like *Best Gay Erotica 2011* and *Best Gay Romance 2010*. He co-wrote the screenplay for the 2009 Joe Gage-directed porn film *Dad Takes a Fishing Trip*. He lives in Pittsburgh, Pennsylvania.

MARK WILDYR has sold over sixty short stories and novellas exploring developing sexual awareness and intercultural relationships to *Freshmen* and *Men* magazines, Alyson, Arsenal, Bold Strokes, Cleis, Companion, Green Candy, Haworth, and STARbooks. He has three published novels: *Cut Hand*, an historical novel; *River Otter*, a sequel; and *The Victor and the Vanquished*, a contemporary story. *Echoes of the Flute* is due out in Spring 2014 and *Charley Blackbear* in Fall 2014. Readers may contact him through his Web site, www.markwildyr.com.

GERARD WOZEK is the author of a book of poems, *Dervish*, and a travel memoir, *Postcards From Heartthrob Town*. Visit him online at www.gerardwozek.com.

Gay Erotica at Its Best

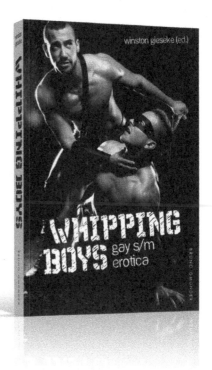

Winston Gieseke (Ed.)
WHIPPING BOYS
Gay S/M Erotica
208 pages, softcover,
13 x 19 cm, 5¼ x 7½",
978-3-86787-689-6
US$ 17.99 / £ 11.99
€ 16,95

Society has long tried to control sexual behavior with shame. But what happens when it's the shame that turns you on? In *Whipping Boys*, desire and domination take on many forms, from spanking and bondage to punishment and humiliation: A dom and his submissive share a special celebration, while a young man discovers what a naughty little pig he can be. Whether you enjoy having your hands tied behind your back or you get off putting someone in his place, this erotic anthology of extreme sex and the men who beg for it will inflict just the right amount of sting. When you fall in love, there's always a chance you'll get hurt ... when you're a whipping boy, it's guaranteed.

Gay Erotica at Its Best

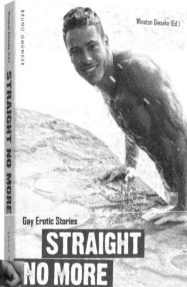

Winston Gieseke (Ed.)
INDECENT EXPOSURES
Gay Erotic Stories
192 pages, softcover,
13 x 19 cm, 5¼ x 7½",
978-3-86787-520-2
US$ 17.99 / £ 11.99 / € 16,95

Winston Gieseke (Ed.)
DADDY KNOWS BEST
Gay Erotic Stories
208 pages, softcover
13 x 19 cm, 5¼ x 7½"
978-3-86787-590-5
US$ 17.99 / £ 11.99 / € 15,95

Winston Gieseke (Ed.)
TEAM PLAYERS
Gay Erotic Stories
208 pages, softcover
13 x 19 cm, 5¼ x 7½"
978-3-86787-609-4
US$ 17.99 / £ 11.99 / € 15,95

Guidebooks for the Curious and Adventurous

Micha Schulze & Christian Scheuss
THE ASS BOOK
Staying on Top of Your Bottom
176 pages, softcover,
13 x 19 cm, 5¼ x 7½",
978-3-86787-525-7
US$ 16.99 / £ 12.99 / € 14,95

Micha Schulze &
Christian Scheuss
THE DICK BOOK
Tuning Your Favorite Body Part
184 pages, softcover,
13 x 19 cm, 5¼ x 7½"
978-3-86787-446-5
US$ 15.99 / £ 11.99 / € 14,95

Micha Schulze & Christian Scheuss
CUM!
The Complete Guide to Orgasm
192 pages, softcover
13 x 19 cm, 5¼ x 7½"
978-3-86787-588-2
US$ 16.99 / £ 12,99 / € 14,95